THE LAST CHILD

Mark Bennett

PublishAmerica
Baltimore

© 2004 by Mark Bennett.

All rights reserved. No part of this book may be reproduced, stored in a retrieval system or transmitted in any form or by any means without the prior written permission of the publishers, except by a reviewer who may quote brief passages in a review to be printed in a newspaper, magazine or journal.

First printing

ISBN: 1-4137-6140-2
PUBLISHED BY PUBLISHAMERICA, LLLP
www.publishamerica.com
Baltimore

Printed in the United States of America

*For Sara and Diana,
whose child eyes never
saw the light of day...*

Prologue

As the visitor stepped into the light, the warm air brushed against his face. He let out a deep breath and began to look at his surroundings. The foliage was very green and beautiful. He had never seen a place so rich in beauty. It seemed to be a perfect ecological state. Glancing skyward, he pondered. The sky was an intense blue with just wisps of clouds that rolled by; it was all very peaceful, the most serene planet he had ever visited.

He began to wander about his new surroundings. As he made his was through the brush he came to a clearing. Pushing the nearby foliage out of the way, he looked upon what was once a great city. He was awestruck as he looked upon its vastness. It seemed to stretch out as far as his eyes could take him. With insatiable curiosity he quickly made his way into it.

Entering, he could see that this city was very old. It was quite an archeological find, actually. The many structures lay crumbling, devoid of all life and upkeep. *There was once a proud race here*, he thought.

As the visitor walked about he came to a building surrounded with many pillars and stairs leading up to it. The majestic building was being overtaken by vegetation growing up and down. However, intrigued nonetheless, he decided to look more closely at it. His curiosity was getting the better of him.

The visitor walked up the many stairs and at the top there looking at him was a statue. It was a statue of an older man sitting in a chair. The man's face was very solemn. The statue appeared in such a way as though he was looking out and watching over things, much like a father would his children. But the statue seemed saddened somehow, having lost some of the awe it once must have held. The vegetation grew around his legs, threatening to overtake his very presence and completely remove from him the magnificence he once held. *They must have been an amazing race, whatever could have happened to them?* he thought.

Walking up to it, he saw some writing that was covered by the vegetation on the base of the statue. He began to pull the foliage back. It was not an easy task, for it seemed that the stone had broken away and the plants had found holes in the cement and began growing inside it. He managed to get most of it off but a lot of the words that were once there were now gone. All that was left was a title and part of a sentence. So he read it softly and aloud. "'Lincoln Memorial…and that government of the people, by the people, and for the people, shall not perish from the earth.'"

A government, apparently they had a structure of ruling class, he thought as he looked up at the building's architecture, and then at the design of the nearby surrounding buildings. Slowly and somewhat thoughtfully, the visitor walked away.

Deciding to continue in this direction, the visitor went to an erected monument. It was the only structure around that had no vegetation on it. However, it was not very attractive looking. Not at all like the other structures and buildings, this was menacing and cold. It was tall and shaped like a giant spike and on it was writing that read:

In Loving Memory of Our Children

Doesn't look like anything to display love, the visitor thought. Not understanding, the visitor began to search around it and found an entranceway that entered into a small alcove. Going inside, he saw a device upon a table that was still functioning. It was powered by some unknown source but it must have been set up specifically for that purpose.

THE LAST CHILD

It had a type of viewing screen, perhaps a sort of communication device. It had several buttons on it: power, play, rewind. "Well, the power is on, I'll try play," he said. The device began to make several strange noises. He suddenly became afraid, that he might be caught in some sort of trap, but the noises soon stopped and the view screen came alive. The picture was that of a man, an old man, with gray hair and round glasses. His whole demeanor depicted one of wisdom from vast intelligence and experience. And yet somewhere behind his eyes were emptiness and a great sorrow. He spoke.

"Hello there. I'm Dr. William Anderson. I can't address you because I'm not really sure who or what you are. However, you are here, and no doubt you are wondering about this place and about me. Well, that is exactly what this series of three disks is for, to tell you about a once proud race known as human.

"Let me start by saying that in all our abilities, it was our own foolishness, our lack of vision that brought us to this nonexistent state. You will find on a separate disk there nearby a brief background of our history."

The visitor looked on the table and saw the other two disks that made up the three. The man on the screen continued, "It is a bloody and disgraceful history, one wretched with tyranny, maliciousness and greed. It was because of this selfishness that man slowly destroyed his environment, and ultimately himself. We did not have the foresight or perhaps we chose to ignore the approach of our demise, but at any rate we took no note of the impending dilemma until it was too late. The earliest warnings came from the later part of the 21st century when miscarriages began to slowly rise. However much we talked about it, people still went about their business as though nothing would happen. This sort of denial was to no avail. Soon we could no longer ignore it, nobody could. It became such a problem that the governments began to realize the crisis and put forth great energies to avoid it.

"Subsequently, they held meetings and talks and there were those of different opinions, liberal and conservative. All the while we were wasting precious time." The man had a rather exasperated expression on his face as his gestures began to become quite emphatic. "Eventually the other nations realized they too had a problem but like all the rest they talked a lot and did little. Finally," he said, his voice growing quite elevated at this point, "when it could no longer be ignored, they decided to do something, but did they peacefully seek help in an effort to achieve mankind's survival? Oh, no! he said sarcastically. "We were all too proud. Instead of pooling together, some saw it as an opportunity for world domination!" he said with his fists clenched. He stood up and pointed a finger at the screen. "The government that could have its citizens still be able to bring forth offspring would be the one left standing!"

At that moment the man began to wheeze rather violently. Slumping into a chair, his breathing irregular, he half said, half gasped the words out, "Just a moment, please," and he sat there breathing in gulps of air. His face was flushed and the lines that bore into his face looked just a little deeper as if he had aged another ten years, and when he continued his voice was a little sadder.

"I was part of a project to bring forth genetically engineered offspring. I was one of a team of six scientists. We were one of the last of our kind because the average age at that point was 46. There were to be no replacements once we were gone, we had to succeed. And we did," he said matter-of-factly.

It seemed at that moment his eyes became slits as he said, "However, it was our own dismal failure as a race to realize we could continue life; instead, we destroyed it, and ourselves." Letting out a large sigh and straightening himself, he said aloud like a tour guide, "Well, you are here now. So let me take you on a journey of what happened. Let me tell you about man's last child."

Chapter 1
The History...

The United States, Michigan, 1975: A local farming accident spreads a deadly drug into the milk supply across the nation. PBB is permanently part of society, and eventually is spread across the world; 16% rise in birth defects.

Soviet Union, 1983: A nuclear accident at Chernobyl causes widespread cancer in six eastern countries of Europe. The result, a defective gene passed on generation after generation.

The world, 1985: Drug and alcohol abuse up 1024% over last ten years. Birth defects and miscarriages 98% of all. Remaining 2% have defective DNA leading to behavior problems.

United States, 1986: Greenpeace marches on Washington for new laws regarding landfills and waste disposal. Greenpeace provides hard-core evidence of sharp increase of disease. Washington quotes loss of money and jobs to Greenpeace proposal; nothing is done.

The world, 1988: The World Health Organization recognizes a new strain of hepatitis. Hepatitis C is born. This strain causes birth defects and miscarriage among all who have been infected.

The world, 1989: Prices in oil, agriculture skyrocket to an inflation high of 10%.

The world, 1992: The World Health Organization recognizes chronic fatigue syndrome as a handicap. CFS inflicts mostly women and causes a miscarriage rate of 50%.

Saudi Arabia, 1993: Missiles fired from Iraq carried biological weaponry. Complete effects upon soldiers and future generations—classified.

The world, 1994: AIDS spreading among third-world countries like wildfire. All experimental drugs have failed. HIV positive births 99.4 %. Death usually within 1-4 years.

United States, 1995: Failure of government to provide good health coverage.

The world, 2015: Prices on agriculture and gas continue to rise due to taxation and governmental power. Middle class dwindling rapidly.

United States, 2016: Domestic violence up 78% from 20 years. Infant death reaching peak of one million per year.

Europe, 2018: Asia and European countries form the new Eastern Alliance. United Nations becoming more like the former League of Nations. US and Canada and Latin countries form Western Alliance.

The world, 2019: Failure of Greenpeace and of nations to adopt a worldwide pollution control solution. Most cities have to adopt a no-drive day due to smog.

The world, 2022: All countries being forced to utilize nuclear fission power. This is due to the amount of pollution in the air from burning of coal. Storage leaks and damages to environment cause widespread depletion of immune system in population.

THE LAST CHILD

The world, 2022: United Nations dissolved. Countries begin building and testing of nuclear warheads.

African Republic, 2023: The world's first nuclear war. Africa and Eastern Alliance have limited exchange in nuclear warheads. Death rate among births 88.5% among all post-war pregnancies.

Industry of China & Chemtech USA 2023: Develop new strain of virus for use in biological weaponry. Tested on population by release into atmosphere. Death rate 68%. Company sued by US citizens. Trial lasted two years and company president sentenced to 12 years imprisonment. He was released after six months for good behavior. Current whereabouts, unknown.

The world, 2024: Middle class dissolved. Most countries under indefinite martial law. All countries using military to enforce even basic civil laws.
  Population of homeless 50%. Most live in shelters.

Acid rain occurring in all major cities. Rationing and purifying done by more affluent countries. Third-world countries are financially unable.

World leaders recognize problem in birth rate, but because of the dissolution of the United Nations they are unsure how to proceed. Most look to use it as an advantage over others.

Infertility rate 60%
Sperm count in men down 72.3%
Miscarriages up 75%
Still births 50%
Sudden infant death syndrome 38%

The world, 2025. First generation of sterile children.

CHAPTER 2

AUGUST 6, 2071

Doug McDowell yawned. It was another day. And yet he was not overjoyed. *But then who is on a work day*, he thought. He stretched and groaned as most men do as they achieve middle age, when the muscles and bones seem to ache just a little more each day. The covers to his bed were a mess from the lack of sleep he seemed to be getting recently.

Hitting the control panel by his bed, he opened the drapes and turned on the coffee pot. The view was nice. As nice as it could be; after all, it was a military base. His home was at the far corner and his view was that of the mountains. He wanted nothing more than to climb those mountains. "I will climb to the top and let out a yell," he said. His smiled faded though for he knew that his dream to get out from behind the walls would never be realized. He was permanently there. It seemed like years ago that he had been brought to the camp. Every day it felt more and more like his prison. It had actually only been a year and they treated him well. He had everything he could ask for, including money, and yet…he was stuck there.

It had been two years ago that he had won the Nobel Prize on his studies of DNA and reassembling of genes from the genetic code. He had felt as if the world had no boundaries and neither did he. He was actually successful in cloning part of human DNA. It was then that the US government became keenly interested in him. But as he later found out, they hired him not only for the reason of being on the genetic project for development of children, it was also for the purpose of not letting a foreign power get to him first, by either offering him to work for them or to assassinate him to prevent him from helping the US.

He had felt, when they offered him the enormous salary including the house and cars, that he had fallen into a gold mine. "Well, I fell all right, right into a gravel pit," he grumbled aloud.

Rubbing his eyes, he then got up and stumbled into the bathroom. "Lights!" he yelled and the computer, hearing his command, turned the light on. Looking into the mirror, he made a face and stuck his tongue out at himself "Yuck!" Frowning, he opened the drawer and got out his electric shaver, toothbrush, comb and set it all down near the sink as he was accustomed to every morning. He turned on the water in the shower and got in. The hot water always felt good on his muscles and back. It was then that the communication link beeped.

"It never fails," he said. He stood there a minute as the water dribbled down on him, not sure if he should bother, yet he knew he better. So he turned the water off and, grabbing a towel, he sat down, faced the screen and turned it on.

A man sat there with a uniform and rank insignia of general. Doug recognized him immediately. "John," he said. He had known the man long enough that he didn't always bother with titles.

"Hello, Doug. It appears I got you out of the shower."

"Uh, slightly," he said, rather annoyed.

"Well, I'm sorry, Doug, but I had to. You better get dressed and get over here to see this. I'll clue you in later," John said with that sense of urgency that Doug knew all too well—trouble.

"I'll be right there," said Doug.

John nodded that stiff informal nod of his and the screen went black.

Doug didn't have two seconds when the door chime rang. "Identify," he said to the computer.

"Col. Rick Stein, US Marine Corps," the voice said.

"He sure didn't waste any time now, did he? Computer, inform him to wait."

"Acknowledged," returned the computer.

Chapter 3

Deep underground in a secret laboratory

Bill Anderson was just amazed. The cellular cohesion was appearing to hold as he gazed down through the microscope. His eyes were sore from looking into the scope, but he didn't care. This was the best thing since the project started. They were going to succeed.

Joan, the lab technician, came bursting into the room with coffee and donuts for him since he hadn't bothered to eat anything in some time.

He didn't appear to notice her, something he did a lot, though she did notice him, there in a white lab coat looking through his microscope at something other than her. She heaved a big sigh. *If only I could get him out of this place it could be different.*

She set the donuts and coffee down. He did not look up. "Are you going to eat anything?" she said more forcefully than she cared to.

"Huh?" he said, not looking up.

She let out an exasperated sigh and, shaking her head, stormed out of the room.

"Did you say something, Joan?" Bill asked after she had already left. He looked up from the microscope. Then realizing the donuts and coffee were there beside him, he quickly ran to the door of the lab and yelled out, "THANK YOU!" She obviously would not hear him, but at least he could say he thanked her. Having now appeased his conscience for his rude behavior, he began to stuff his face with the donuts, gulping down the coffee between breaths.

He hadn't realized how hungry he really was until he started to eat. *How long has it been now, two days maybe?* He sighed. He thought of Joan as he finished eating. She seemed like a really nice person. She was very attractive, very shapely and very intelligent, having graduated from Harvard at age seventeen with a master's degree. Perhaps someday he would get to know her better.

When I have more time, he thought. He let out a sigh, his chin coming to rest on his hand. He suddenly jerked up realizing he was daydreaming. He looked around quickly to see if anyone noticed, blushing until his cheeks were a bright pink, which was heightened by his blond hair.

He let out a sigh in relief, realizing that he was alone in the lab. He hadn't enough sleep, he hadn't enough of anything. *That includes socializing*, his thoughts drifting back to Joan. *Someday*, he thought again, *when I have more time....* His face contorted into a scowl. "Time is the problem, isn't it, for everyone!" he said aloud to nobody.

He then walked across the lab to speak with the computer. It was there that they kept all the information accumulated thus far. It was also the computer that controlled the various machines for their experiments.

He smiled to himself before doing anything with the computer, thinking one hundred years ago or so the thought of a talking computer or talking to one had seemed preposterous, maybe even annoying to some. But with the new personality computers, in which they built a human subroutine inside the machine to make it seem more alive, it was possible and a definite plus. And the institute's Genetic Engineering Order computer—GEO for short—was certainly no exception.

"Hello GEO," Bill said.

"Hello, Dr. Anderson," it replied in a soft-spoken male voice. "And what may I do for you?"

"I want to access the files on the brain and central nervous system, specifically the cellular cohesion data," said Bill.

"Accessing..." the computer said.

It was at that moment that Doug came into the room.

"Doug! Come take a look at this," Bill said, grabbing Doug by the arm and pulling him to the microscope to examine the sample.

"What, what!" Doug said, pulling his arm from Bill's grasp and dropping all his files and papers that he had spent an hour the night before arranging.

"The cell, it's dividing!" said Bill with a glint of joy that Doug had not seen in a long time.

Doug's jaw dropped open. With a glimmer of hope in his eyes, he shoved passed Bill, walking right across the papers he had dropped and looked through the microscope.

"Can it be?" he asked, looking up at Bill. "It worked?" He already knew the answer himself because he was looking at the proof. He just needed to hear someone say it aloud.

Bill leaned in closer to him and said with a big smile that could light up the entire room, "It worked!"

They both stood there staring at each other, not having anything to say, both so stunned. Then at the same time they let out a yell of joy, hugging each other and laughing and crying at the same time. All the frustration, time, and aggravation was letting itself out all at once in a moment of pure elation.

Joan was finally coming off of duty at the base. Between servicing the geneticists and her own work she was extremely tired. *Getting up every day at some god-awful hour, coming into the lab, sitting behind the computer all day, looking at the endless amount of genetic code that spews from the computer*, she said, grumbling to herself. *Looking up everything the geneticists want, when they want it.*

Sometimes I'd like to tell them where they can shove their genetic code, she said to herself, as she walked away from her work. She turned down two corridors to the left and walked up to the door of her stateroom. It was small compared to the geneticists'. They got to have houses.

Well, the grass is always greener, eh, Joan, she said to herself. She knew full well, though, it was far better than the rest of the world.

She put her ID card in the code slot. The door opened with a swoosh. She walked inside. The room was a mess. She had food still on the table from last night's party. She had managed to get some of the people to stop all their busy work and come over for a little traditional beer and pizza. Once the party really got going they started some beer games, and well, they were pretty wasted by the time she kicked them all out early that morning.

Looking around she thought, *Oh God.* The thought of cleaning up was almost too much to bear. Her headache from the party seemed to come back in that instant at the thought of cleaning up. She sat down on one of the chairs in her Victorian-styled room. She had a wonderful collection of art and literature as well as beautiful Victorian furniture. Having some nice things was one of the perks of working for the government.

She pulled herself off the chair and walked down the hallway to her bathroom where she grabbed the pain killers that she had taken for her hangover that morning. Her headache had returned. She got a glass and gulped down three pills. She was just about to go into the bedroom to sleep for a while when she heard the yell.

Kirk was on patrol duty that morning as he was every morning. He was dressed in his full army camouflage, ready to do battle with the enemy regardless of whom that may be, and to protect the people that he was there to protect, namely the scientists. He was proud to be there, proud of his uniform and proud to be an American. He held the rank of sergeant major and he had a full brigade under his command. He could have had others doing the rounds for him, but he wanted the men to see him there with them. It would keep their morale high, which he felt was critical at all times.

At that instant, a yell went up from the lab like one he had never heard. Quickly pulling his gun from his belt, he bolted down the corridor, not sure of what he would find. As he ran, other soldiers fell in behind him running as well. When they got down to where the lab was, Joan came from around the other corridor.

"Dr. Tate, look out!" He jumped in front of her, bumping her out of the way, and at the same time sliding into the lab with his gun raised.

Bill and Doug stopped their jumping up and down as everyone came bursting though the door. Suddenly realizing they were holding one another and that people were looking, they let go of one another, embarrassed.

"Oh, I'm sorry, doctors," Kirk said, lowering his gun as he realized he must look pretty silly to come charging in like the charge of the light brigade, but hell it was his job. "Is everything OK?" he asked.

Nodding his head, realizing that a gun was pointed at him, Bill stammered, "Yes, quite."

Bill was about to dismiss the soldiers when Joan, pushing her way past the soldiers, including the one who had held her back from entering the lab when Kirk went in, made her way to the fore. Her hair was a mess and in her face. She was hot and angry because she had assessed the situation as soon as she had come in the door.

Other colleagues had come into the room, all wondering what had happened. Joan spoke up and said rather testily, "Everything's fine now that John Wayne has the situation under control," looking Kirk straight in the eye.

"Just doing my job the best way I know how," Kirk replied stiffly.

"A little too well, don't you think?" Joan said.

"It's OK, Joan," Doug said. "I'm glad we have someone that is this concerned with our safety."

"Well, now that we are all here," she said with a frown on her face and her voice a bit sharp, "do you mind telling us what the hell is going on?"

"It's going to work," Doug said. He then grabbed Joan by the shoulders and enthusiastically said, "It's going to work!"

It was then that everyone let out a cheer of joy, all congratulating each other, all but Bill, of course. Standing up on the table, he whistled to get everyone's attention.

"We still have to compile the data in the computer with the data that Dr. Tate has provided to get a yes or no. GEO is working on that right now," he said, gesturing toward the computer. "But, people, please, I need to stress to you the need to keep this under wraps. This information is not to get out." He looked directly at Doug.

Doug smiled rather sheepishly. Bill understood though. This was the best news that had come through this place since the project began. Doug now spoke up. "He's right, until that data is done this project is still under wraps. I want all to consider this a forbidden subject."

Everyone was still in quite an emotional state. Some were happy, some had mixed emotions, some were dumbfounded. But whatever the feeling the individuals had, all were feeling their spirits lift from the edgy state they were all in.

Bill motioned to Pam. "Pam, I want you to get General John Bass on the comlink. I would like Doug and Sgt. Major Kirk to attend. As far as the rest of you…" he paused just long enough to see if he had their attention as well as to lock eyes with each of them, "you have your orders. Dismissed."

Although they had been given stern orders as they filtered out of the lab, a general feeling of hope and joy seemed to glow out of each one.

Chapter 4

September 14, 2071
African Republic, somewhere deep underground

General Hussad was accompanied by his soldiers to the genetic testing lab. This was to be it. Finally, his country would rise to supreme power. He would crush the other nations, and he alone would hold the key to life and death for all. But there would be no life for them, because they did not practice the sacred way of the Afim.

He was dressed in a white uniform with many decorations pinned on. He marched in front of his row of men. Each soldier saluted him. They gave him the honor that was much deserved by him, for he was a great man in their eyes. One to rise to power and finally show the world, the Christian world, that theirs was the only way.

The world called him a madman; they said he was worse then Adolph Hitler. He did horrible things to people, even his own. Now they would all be made to understand. They would be forced to admit that he was God's prophet. They would see His light shining upon him when he revealed his prophecy of just Afim occupying the world.

The men were stiffly saluting. Their faces were like stone. Their discipline, impenetrable. Hussad soaked it all in. The thought of failure could not be further from his mind. They knew the price of failure: death, and not at all pleasantly.

He stopped just short of the door, turned around, and looked at everyone. He caught each man's eyes, fixing them for a moment as he savored his triumph. Taking in a deep breath, he walked through the lab doors and into the lab.

Hussad stopped short just inside the doorway. Looking down the stairs and into the lab, Hussad saw Hadeen on his knees in front of him. Hussad realized instantly what at happened. There was only one reason that Hadeen would be in such a position—if he had failed. The initial shock of seeing this was like a brick wall. Now his blood was about to boil over like a volcano erupting.

"Failure!" he said with his mouth now hanging open. Hussad's look was the look of a man who had just been slapped. The initial shock, the feeling of embarrassment and pain, then his face began to contort into one of rage.

Bolting down the stairs, he knocked Hadeen over with a blow to his head. Hadeen went reeling backwards and let out a cry as the wind was knocked out of him. His head was swooning and the room was spinning even though he was lying down.

Hussad grabbed him by the hair, picking him up. His hand went around Hadeen's throat, as he began to lift him off the ground by the neck.

Still holding him, "Guard!" he yelled in the direction of the door. The soldiers came bursting in and took up a firing position against the scientists.

Calling one of the soldiers over to him, Hussad ordered him to bring him the experiment.

The soldier walked to where Hadeen had lain the remains down. Picking up the remains of the child, the soldier took a moment to glance at it once. The flesh only partially grown, it had taken eight and a half months to get to this point and yet this experiment too had ended in failure.

The soldier brought the child to Hussad who looked at it and very soberly nodded. The soldier then removed the remains.

Hussad spoke slowly, with a very hushed tone, almost with a hiss. He said to the man in his grasp, "What happened?"

"The exp…" seemed to be all he could muster as Hussad slammed him against the wall. Hussad's face was only a fraction away from the man's. His breathing was hard. Gripping the man tightly, he screamed, "What happened!"

"The matrix would not hold and…" was all the man could muster.

"Wouldn't hold…" Hussad said mockingly. "WOULDN'T HOLD!!!" Hussad screamed. Hussad was shaking the man by his throat. All the while the man was gasping for air. Hussad began pounding his head into the wall until there was a smear of blood on the wall. Hadeen's head was slumped over Hussad's hand. Blood was oozing from his mouth. Hussad flung the body from him. Spitting toward it, he yelled, "Idiot!"

The other three scientists were now completely bent over with their faces to the floor, sniffling. Hussad became silent, as though he was in deep thought, such as when one is praying. The silence did not last long. He whirled around quickly as if the rage that had taken him before might grip him again.

He jerked up the nearest young scientist by the collar. Eyeing him, he said matter-of-factly, "Tell me why I should not kill you?"

The other scientist blurted out all the reasons why he thought he could do the job better. He said that the team was going in the wrong direction and if he was leader it would work. He said anything he could to discredit Hadeen and make himself look better, hoping beyond all hope that it was enough. The other scientists looked up and began to agree and nod their heads in approval.

Hussad let out a sigh. He sat down in a chair and studied the man's face for a long hard moment. He studied all their faces.

It was at that time a soldier carrying an envelope came up and saluted to him. "Sir, intelligence report," the soldier said, holding out the envelope.

Hussad saluted back and took the envelope from the soldier. The soldier turned and walked out as Hussad opened the envelope. There was a long silent moment as Hussad read the report. He nodded slowly to himself.

The young scientist was sweating bricks. He was praying that the letter contained some good news, anything that might improve the general's mood. Unfortunately for him, it was not good news.

Hussad put the report back in the envelope and put it in his pocket. He looked at the group of young scientists. "It seems that the Americans have succeeded in producing a child."

The scientist's hopes were dashed. The young scientist's heart felt as though it would burst from all the adrenaline coursing though his veins. Trying one last-ditch effort, he said, "If you give us another chance, we too can succeed."

Hussad never answered. He headed for the door and addressed one of his soldiers. He instructed him to have his top advisor meet him at the table for lunch. Saluting stiffly, the soldier left.

Hussad stopped just short of the door, looked at his other soldiers and said, "Bring them."

The soldiers grabbed the remaining three up off the floor, dragging and pushing them forward. They all thought, *This is it*. They did not know what was going to happen as Hussad took them across the hall and into another restricted area that none of them had ever seen.

The young scientist's hopes began to rise once again. They had never been in this area, perhaps they were just going to be reassigned. They came into a control room.

Hussad now addressed them. "This is our new phased energy technology."

The scientists looked through the glass watching the beams of light. They streaked across the room hitting some unknown target.

Looking at the beam, Hussad spoke in a very hushed, thoughtful voice, "We hope to create a very powerful weapon in the future." Turning to face them, he added, "Right now we have it cutting eight-by-eight steel slabs into one-by-one squares. You see the beam goes through a splitter and cuts three slabs of steel at once."

The scientists' eyes went wide as they caught the sick irony. Hussad turned off the machine, pulled the safety key out of the control panel and handed it to the nearest soldier. He looked at the soldier and nodded his head in the direction of the energy machine.

The soldier didn't need verbal orders to understand what he was to do. He knew his duty and he was going to carry it out. He gestured to his fellow soldiers and they pushed the scientists off toward the door that led inside the chamber. Their screams could be heard by Hussad as he walked out the door.

Walking away from the building, he quickly let his demeanor turn to one of pleasantry. He walked into the tent where food, drinks, and beautiful servant girls were aplenty. He was handed a drink from one of the servants as he sat down across from his advisor. Smiling to him as he held up his glass, he spoke. "If I can't have good technology, I'll get some better scientists, or better yet, let's forget the scientists and steal the technology."

The other man just grinned at him.

Chapter 5

November 24, 2071
Eastern Alliance

General Polov was pacing. *The alliance has to make a decision about the current situation with the United States,* he thought. *Surely such smugness on the part of the US will not go without retribution. They must know that by blatantly denying that the experiment of the child even exists, they are asking for war.*

This is at least what Polov hoped for. He had long believed now that world government could only be achieved by world domination. Dominate the strong players and the other nations would fall into line—that was his philosophy. Polov threw up his hands. "What is taking the bureaucrats so long!" he said aloud.

Polov sat down on his couch in his living room, picked up the remote and turned on some music. Beethoven was especially good when Polov was having an anxiety attack, or when he was in a foul mood. He was in both, although the music did little to calm him. He turned off the music, threw the remote down and began his persistent pacing.

In amongst his pacing and his grumbling, the comm beeped. Polov more dived into the chair at his desk than sat in it, hitting the button on the comm and revealing the Secretary of the Alliance.

"Mr. Secretary," he said, acknowledging the man.

"General Polov, the alliance has reached a decision. Your recommendations for the use of military force have been approved. Your orders are as follows: you are to assemble an insurmountable force of unprecedented power, together with full military strategies for deployment of such. It seems if we cannot have the technology, we will take it by force. We will have war for the preservation of our culture."

Polov was stoic. His military training helped him to keep his emotions hidden from all. However, inside, he was thrilled. This was what he had wanted all along.

"Yes, sir, it shall be done," Polov said.

"Good. You are to report to me tomorrow at the Alliance bunker at 0800 hours. There you will give a presentation to the Alliance of our military strategy. You have much to do tonight, I suggest you get started immediately."

"It will be ready, Mr. Secretary," Polov answered.

The screen went blank, but Polov was all lit up inside.

November 25, 2071
8:00 a.m.
Alliance headquarters, deep underground

Polov's heart was racing as he walked through the hallways of the underground caverns. He was being escorted by a lieutenant. Their footsteps echoed off the cement floor as well as the pipes lining the cement walls. The sound was driving Polov mad. Although he had been there before, he was, after all, the senior officer and reported to the Alliance on a regular basis. This time though was different. The Alliance's victory, his own victory, was finally at hand. He could go down as one of the greatest generals in history.

The more he thought about it the more his anxiousness grew. He wanted nothing more than to run down the rest off the hallway and burst into the room to get the political formality out of the way. However, he kept himself under control; he and the lieutenant continued to walk down the many hallways.

"Alliance members," the first secretary spoke. "Today is a red letter day in our history. As you are aware, our attempts up to this point in genetic engineering of a human have failed. Our scientists believe that it is at least a decade away. As you are all aware, based upon the current age group of our population, as well as the current environmental degradation, ten years or more is an unacceptable amount of time.

"You are also aware that we are not alone in our efforts. Many nations continue to work on such projects. However, as we have already learned, the United States has been successful in its attempts to create a genetically stable and healthy child. Even now it grows in their laboratory. Our operatives have confirmed this information.

"We have dispatched not just one but three ambassadors, on three separate occasions, to the United States in order to come to some understanding, maybe even friendship, if we at all can. However, it would seem that when confronted about sharing the technology, the US government suddenly gets a case of amnesia. Their own President denied it directly to my face. This is an intolerable act. It is an act of war!" He pounded his fist down on the table.

The first secretary's tone became harsh and he began to pace back and forth in front of the delegation as he spoke. "This act is not by a military force," he said with his arms gesturing wide, "but by mass genocide of our culture! Therefore, if death is what they would choose for us, we shall rain death down upon them! It shall be war!" he yelled as his fist slammed down upon the conference table.

No one flinched during this emotional but effective speech by the secretary. They were all too caught up in their own emotions and nationalistic feelings at that moment. They needed no convincing, for they were the ones that had made the decision for war the day before. The secretary was merely recapping what had taken place.

Polov could hear the whole speech from outside. *C'mon, c'mon, wrap it up*, he thought impatiently.

"I have here with us General Polov," the first secretary said.

That was Polov's cue to come inside. Polov threw open the doors and walked into the chamber to the head of the delegation.

Polov stood by the first secretary in his usual respectful way, to the right and a little behind him, his face impassive, showing none of the elation that he held inside, although his elation was starting to get to him. *If he keeps talking I will pitch him out the window*, Polov thought.

"The general will brief us on our current military strategy….General," he said as he yielded the floor to Polov.

The general took his place in front of the delegates. "Mr. Secretary, members of the Alliance, you have heard the recap and are aware of our current defense position, so I will come right to it. What I propose is this…." Taking out a device from his pocket, he pointed it at the table. "If you observe, please, the center of the table." At that moment the table center slid aside to reveal a map of the world. "As you can see, these are the locations of our current troop deployment," he said, pointing to the various red blips on the screen. "I suggest a full strike into the heart of North America by concentrating our ground forces to march through Canada. This will draw the United States into a conventional war. As the enemy brings his forces from the south and attempts to build some form of defense, we will attack from his southwestern border. Our paratroops from the province of Britain will then begin the attack upon the base itself while our operatives from within the base will then secure the data necessary for us, as well as any children, if they can. Once our objective is met we will immediately go to the bargaining table to ask for their unconditional surrender. That is, of course, unless the Americans are easily thwarted whereupon our forces shall gain easy victory."

"Ahem, General, if I may." One Englishman had his hand raised. "What makes you think that the Americans will be so easily thwarted as you say, or that they might surrender so easily? Canada might be weak but the US is not. Neither are they just going to let you fly up to their southwest border and say, here I am, don't mind if I send my paratroopers over, do you?"

The general smiled. He had anticipated all their questions; after all, they made policy but he made war and he had not gotten to where he was by not being good at anticipating the other person.

"The southwest border is patrolled by three main bases or hubs as it were." Utilizing a pointer, he began to show the areas on North

THE LAST CHILD

America. He pointed to California as he spoke. "The main hubs are here, here and here," pointing to each location. "We have been sending troops this way through their own immigration office, as though they were all seeking supposed defection. We have also been smuggling weapons, piece by piece, mostly through things like oil freighters; the oil kept the components safe and no one suspected. Then over the course of a few years we had all the components reassembled.

"We then began to seek out some of their own disgruntled citizens, who wanted to see their federal government go down long ago. We have four platoons and three nuclear devices all ready to go on Project Jackal. As soon as we begin, these three bases will be taken out of commission. This will send confusion to the rest of the military regarding communication because, as you can no doubt see, there is nobody around to tell about it. By the time they become aware of what has happened, it will be too late. The ground war will have begun and no one will realize that we have paratroopers in their southwest corner."

Taking a deep breath and straightening his tunic, he continued, "Now, once we have seized the base, their technology becomes ours. We become their life blood, so to speak. They can die on the battlefield or they can take our terms and live through their children. We shall then transfer the Alliance flag there and then we shall have achieved two victories. One, the preservation of our race, and two, a single world government. That, ladies and gentlemen, is what I propose."

Everyone was silent. Polov could begin to feel the sweat on the back of his neck making the collar that he wore so tightly become irritable. He pulled on his collar. He was about to try to add something, but as he started to open his mouth to speak the secretary rose. He began to clap, slowly at first and then faster. Then all the people began to clap.

The general grinned, for he had won.

Chapter 6

"Oh, isn't he just beautiful?" Joan said.

"Yes, he is!" exclaimed Doug, as he was grinning from ear to ear, tapping at the glass.

"What do you think we should name him?" asked Bill.

Nobody spoke at that moment to answer the question for they were all to busy admiring the wonderful sight that was before them—a baby. They all wanted to touch him, but there was a protective casing around him, much like an incubator. They had various monitors hooked to the baby and an IV in its arm, but despite all the cold equipment, there was a little life that reached out and grabbed their innermost parts and made them glow. He looked up at everyone and captured everyone's heart all over again.

However, business as always, Bill quickly recovered. "Alright, everyone, let's break it up. We all have work to do," said Bill

"Aw," everyone groaned and griped but they all began to move away.

Doug smiled. Bill was so predictable, even during happy occasions. The man was all business. He would stop, occasionally, to smell the roses, but only for a moment, then he was right back to his intense business demeanor, and from the looks of him, now was one of those times. "Well, what's up? Everyone seems to be pleased but you."

Taking Doug by the arm, Bill began to walk down the hallway. Doug could tell that Anderson was troubled. "Doug, do you know anything about children?" asked Bill solemnly.

The grin on Doug's face was replaced with a look of absolute dumbfoundedness. It had never occurred to him. They had all been so busy worrying about whether or not they could procreate, nobody had considered taking care of the child once they had it. They had touched on it in the beginning, but that had been years ago, and as time progressed, more and more emphasis was put on research for the actual experiment.

Looking at Bill, Doug said, "Well, I...."

In the middle of Doug's stuttering, Pam came bursting in the room with fresh coffee and donuts.

Seeing Pam, Bill and Doug stood in the room staring at the donuts and coffee, as if their minds were a million miles away, but their bodies said, "Feed me!"

Pam looked at both of them and said, "Ah, anybody hungry?"

That question seemed to snap them both back to the present. "Ah, yes, yes, Pam, thank you very much for doing this," Doug said as they both walked back into the room.

"Well now, I thought that this occasion required a celebration," Pam said.

"With coffee and donuts?" said Doug, remembering that Joan's celebrations were a little bit more intense than Pam's.

"This would be a celebration for me if you two would eat a little bit from time to time." She took Bill's clipboard from his hand and replaced it with a mug of coffee. She then gave Doug a jelly donut, and they ate and drank obediently. Pam nodded and said, "Good."

Pam walked over to the glass case where the baby was. The baby was awake and Pam started to make a big silly face at the baby and talk to it. "Hi, hello there, you are so precious. My name is Pam. We are going to have so much fun...." Pam began to coo at the child.

The child's eyes were an intense blue and he watched every move that Pam made, every gesture and sound.

"Oh, can't we take this thing off of him? He needs to be held, not stuck in a glass case like a piece from a museum," she said exasperatingly as she begun looking for a way to get into the apparatus.

In the background, as Pam was carrying on, Doug and Bill had stopped eating and were watching the whole scene very intently, turning to look at one another with a gleam in their eyes.

Pam opened the top, pulled out the IV, picked the baby up and snuggled the child to her. The baby responded in like manner, and just like a mother bonds with her child, Pam felt instant love for the precious little package that was God-given to her at that moment.

"Um, Pam," Doug said.

"Oh, I'm sorry, Dr. McDowell." Pam was suddenly self-conscious that she had messed with the experiment and quickly put the child back into the case and re-hooked the IV up and shut the lid.

The baby began to cry, because it wanted. It did not understand or know what its needs were, but it just knew it wanted something—comfort.

Pam had started to walk towards Doug, and when the child began to cry, she looked back at the baby and then again at Doug, giving him both a hopeful and exasperated look at the same time. "You can't just let that continue," she said rather testily.

"No, no, please," Doug said, gesturing back toward the child.

Pam smiled, quickly moving to the baby, opened the lid and took the baby out. She then snuggled the child to her as she softly spoke to it. "Shhh, Shhh, it's ok, I am here." The child was quickly contented. Pam kissed his little fuzzy head.

Doug came and, standing next to Pam with his arms folded and grinning, looked at Bill. "You were saying, Dr. Anderson?"

Bill smiled in spite of himself. "I was saying that, Pam, we have a very, very special assignment for you."

The old man stopped his recap at that point with a fit of coughing. This time, however, it was with such a hoarseness in his chest that the visitor could not imagine that he could go on. He wished that he could reach in his bag and pull out some medical gear for the old man, but alas he could not. The old man had some form of breathing apparatus on now, holding up his hand in a signal to say just a moment. The visitor wondered why did he not just pause the recording while he got himself together. Perhaps he couldn't or he was trying to make a statement about his condition.

The old man stopped coughing and took the mask off. He smiled faintly and said rather hoarsely, "Well, where…" He stopped short because his voice sounded terrible. Holding his hand up to indicate again that he would be just a moment, he took a swallow of some type of drink that had a rather greenish tint.

"Ah," he said, "nothing like some good water to take care of that hoarseness. Now, where were we?" he said, rubbing his chin. "Oh yes, while this was going on…."

Chapter 7

They all began to filter out of the room after working out all the details of the invasion laid out by Polov. All of them except the one with most of the questions—Bozinov. He sat in the room staring off into space and with his hand on his head; it was all he could do to keep from crying.

"The fools, the fools!" he said aloud to himself. "Thirty years of service to the CIA and just when I am looking to retire this just had to come up!" He had hoped just this one time, he could raise enough questions and paint the US strong enough to avert war, but yet he could not. They are bent on their constant thirst for power. *The worst of it being that they are going to kill over a little child when they know that this could be solved diplomatically. Thirty days till I retire and this is the mission I dread most....*

He thought about his family, his wife, and how much he loved to be with her. It would be so great to go home again. Only this time he would not be getting any secret phone calls; no meetings or worries or being called away on secret missions, just him and Lorraine. He smiled to himself as he remembered the look on her face when he had given her that diamond necklace.

Sighing heavily, he came back to the present. He was going to have to protect them. He began to think over the events of that morning's meeting. He went over it plan by plan, committing it to memory so he could recite it when necessary. He did not dare leave out any details lest something be overlooked.

When he had finished mulling it all over, he drew in a deep breath and let it out. He began to think of the soldiers from the Eastern Alliance flooding though the streets with guns, killing people in their wake, and Lorraine....*My god! What about Lorraine...I have to stop this.* "I will stop this!" he said, looking up, his head high and determination in his eyes. "Well," he said, standing up and squaring his shoulders. "Time to get to work."

He walked out of the room knowing what he had to do. Leaving the building, he hailed a guard to escort him back to his quarters for it was far too dangerous outside. He would take the underground tunnels that linked his building with the others and his home. *Everything perfectly natural*, he thought.

When he reached his door, he thanked the guard, saluted him and dismissed him just as he did every night.

Bozinov closed the door behind him, taking his coat off. He did not bother to hang it up, he just draped it over the nearest chair as he walked though the house. He was careful not to mutter any words aloud because listening devices were standard security for all officials. This way the Alliance ensured their loyalty. However, Bozinov was an old pro. Turning to the wall monitor, he put on the daily news. He then made sure that the sound level was loud enough to drown out any noise, but not too loud so as to attract suspicion. He went into his bedroom, and kneeling down beside the bed, removed the grill from the wall vent to the heating and cooling duct. The next part, however, was his feat of genius. He smiled to himself because it was really inventive.

Anyone could look inside the vent but no one would think to remove the screws from the duct work, sliding one of the panels off, revealing the area between the duct and the insulation. When he took the panel off, there was an area just large enough for a small box.

They will never find this. He smiled to himself. Removing the box, he had to work fast for it was always dangerous; if anyone were to come in the door it would be all over.

He opened the box, removing two devices and a cable. He took them out of his bedroom and into the study where his desk and computer were. He turned the computer around and disconnected the network cable from behind it. This cable served as a security measure so that a higher-ranking official could view files on others' computers to see what they are doing. This, of course, again ensured their loyalty.

They made big claims about their security, but the truth was that they did not have the time nor the resources to constantly check it out. He had done this many times without getting caught, and if he ever did, he would just break the cable and reattach it claiming he had accidentally broke it by stepping on it with the chair while rocking. It would sound ridiculous, but it would be most believable. If the story made sense that was when there would be cause for suspicion.

He finished disconnecting the cable and quickly typed out the message:

ID 45DT7ZGB9
INVASION U.S. IMMINENT GAIN CONTROL OF ADAM

That was all he dared to type, for anything more would be easily recognizable.

He then took the cable that he had brought out of the box and plugged the one end into the device and the other end into the network port on the computer. The computer would think he was just sending a document through the network, but it would actually be sending it to the device.

He sent the file and then erased the log file that showed that a document had been sent. He disconnected the cable and erased all traces from the computer about the document he had typed.

He then re-hooked the network cable and, taking the device with the information on it, walked over to the wall monitor. This had to be the greatest feat of scientific genius. He would use the monitor to piggyback the decoded message with the newscast.

However, just as he finished the cable hookups, the power went out. "Damn!" he said aloud. "I can't believe this!"

Just as he said that, the power went on again for a few seconds and then off. There was quite a storm going on outside, and it had apparently taken out the power.

He had to think quickly. He needed to get the information out as quickly as possible, as well as get himself out of there. He took a moment to ponder then, moving quickly, he walked over to the communications console and made flight plans to the United Kingdom.

Meanwhile, in another building, Polov and several other officers had been monitoring him....

"His power has been disconnected, sir. It seems he just made flight plans to the United Kingdom," an officer said to Polov.

Polov had suspected Bozinov for some time and the recent conference had allowed him to flush him out. However, it was a great risk to allow Bozinov such freedoms. Had this been any other time he would have thrown him in jail or had him shot, depending upon his mood.

However, these were not normal times. He had to not only win a war but make sure that all the resisters were eliminated. This way he could be sure that after the war was over, an organized resistance wasn't already up and functioning. By allowing Bozinov some maneuverability, he could pick off all those that were associated with him. Still it was a gamble; he could not allow the Americans to have access to his plan, that would be disastrous, not only for the war but himself as well. He had to be sure he played the cat and mouse game very well.

Polov wondered what Bozinov was up to and if he was going to get information out of the Alliance. "Have him followed but not too close. I want to know the whole story before we arrest him."

The other officer nodded. "Yes, sir."

Polov began to walk out and then stopped and turned around, rubbing his chin with the look on his face of a man deep in thought. "Get me the Hunter. I want to meet him in one hour."

"Yes, sir," the officer replied.

With that, Polov turned and walked out.

Chapter 8

November 26, 2071
10:00 p.m.

Bozinov arrived at the airport. He had only one bag with a change of clothes and his communication devices. Walking up to the desk, he checked his bag and picked up his ticket, thanking the woman behind the desk as he went down the hall.

He did not notice the person sitting in a chair reading the newspaper. However, that person noticed him. He got up and walked over to the desk and asked for a ticket on the flight that Bozinov was on. The girl informed him that there was no more room on the flight and that she could get him on another.

However, before she could finish her speech, he pulled out some identification and said, "I will be on that flight."

The girl was surprised for a moment; however, security personnel were a bit of a norm, so gaining her composure, she got him a ticket in first class and bumped someone else.

As soon as the agent left the counter, she began to take a mental note of his appearance, as well as anything he had, for she too was an agent.

The CIA frequently put informants at the airport to monitor security movements. She had recognized Bozinov's name immediately.

She knew that he was an operative, although she had never met him. She knew he was being followed but she wondered if he knew.

She had to make a decision. Perhaps Bozinov wanted the man to follow him to prove that there was nothing wrong with him. Maybe he didn't know or maybe he did know. She was about to pull her hair out when she just decided to get a message to him. Typing on her computer terminal, she quickly brought up another screen that had nothing to do with flight information.

The CIA had one of its network nodes right on the computer system at the airport. From there they could access just about anything. The chances of someone knowing about it were slim, because so many people and businesses utilized it. No one would suspect that they would use such an obvious security risk.

She typed up the charts of another operative at the airport in London and sent him a message about Bozinov's situation.

A person came up to the counter where she was standing. Her senses became heightened, because if someone found out she would have to act fast. However, it was more likely just another paying customer.

"One moment please," she said to the man standing at the desk.

Her computer terminal was below the desk and he could not see what she was doing. She could have had one of her co-workers take him if she had not been alone that day; the other girl had called in sick. However, on reflection, it was probably best that she did. She could not be typing if someone else was lurking around.

She finished the document and hit the send key. She then quickly killed that window, pulling the flight information back up. *Ah, business as usual*, she thought.

Looking up at the gentleman waiting patiently, she asked, "May I help you?"

Bozinov settled into his chair on the airplane. It only took about twenty minutes to get from Moscow to London because the plane actually went up into space, where it could travel much faster, and then back down again. The longest part of the trip was waiting to get clearance to get off the runway. He pulled his hat over his head and fell fast asleep. It was going to be a big day tomorrow.

Unknown to Bozinov, sitting down the aisle and across from him was his nemesis, the Hunter. The man was tall and thin, he wore his hair short and his face well shaven. He had on a black suit and tie, with highly polished shoes and an expensive watch on his wrist. He looked all the part of an important business man ready to be CEO of a company. There were many that looked like him on the plane, all their faces showing little concern for anything as they read their newspapers or business magazines. You could just tell they spent a lot of time on planes. It was what made the Hunter so good at what he did. He just blended in, and you never saw him when he came for you.

The plane began its assent upward until finally it broke through the upper atmosphere. It was the part a lot of the passengers liked because of the weightlessness, but the Hunter did not smile. He did not look out the window, he just continued to be nonchalant, minding his own business. He was to follow Bozinov to his destination, where he would meet up with another trailer, and he would hand over the job to him so as not to tip Bozinov off.

Bozinov woke up with the bump of the plane when the landing gear hit the ground. Grabbing his coat, he got off the plane. He was greeted, as was everyone else, and escorted to the desk where he would show the claims to his baggage.

He walked up to the desk and a well-dressed young man took his claim checks and proceeded to type him into the computer. Bozinov waited patiently when the young man looked up and said, "You are all set, sir." He handed Bozinov his claims back, but on the top of them, on a torn-off scribbled piece of paper, it read, *You are being followed!*

Bozinov just stared at the piece of paper. He was in shock because he had never thought that he would be suspected. This, of course, was his own arrogance and he realized it then. He thought of his retirement, of his wife….The young man, realizing that Bozinov was gaping at the paper, cleared his throat and asked him if there was anything wrong with his claim.

Snapping back to reality, he said, "No, thank you very much."

The young man nodded and Bozinov picked up his bag and walked on.

At the same time, the spy that had followed him met up with his partner. The two exchanged a few words and the one from the airplane left, leaving his partner to take charge.

Bozinov walked out of the airport and hailed a cab. He had to push his way through the many street walkers and homeless people asking him for some money. He managed to get into the car unscathed and instructed the driver to take him to the Riviera in London.

Bozinov was still disturbed about being followed. All of him wanted to turn around and look, but he knew he dared not. He had devoted most of his life to not being detected, so he had not prepared himself for being detected.

He talked to himself, "I must calm down." He began to think about a new plan and the possibility that he may get caught. The first thing he had to do was not let his trailer know he is on to him. He also had to let his contact know that he had a trailer. This he could do at the hotel.

The cab pulled up to the hotel and Bozinov paid the man. The rain began to come down outside just as Bozinov came into the door. It was a beautiful hotel done it late 21st-century decor. There was a great chandelier in the center of the room that hung from the ceiling, a brass railing for the stairs. He wondered how many of the people on the street never saw a sight like this or would be totally dumbfounded if you were to describe it to them.

He walked up to the front desk. This was where he knew he had to get the word out. He also had to get it right, for if he didn't, they would not respond.

"Can I help you, sir?" asked the man behind the desk.

"I would like a suite please, though I prefer suite number five," said Bozinov. There was, of course, no suite number five. That was just the code for saying he needed a contact.

"I'm afraid suite number five is occupied right now," said the man.

"It is more occupied than you think," said Bozinov. "I'll take anything you got."

The man handed him a key and Bozinov moved toward the elevator as the man brought up his communication screen.

Bozinov pushed the button to the elevator and entered after the door had opened. Looking at the controls, he selected which floor he wished to go to, and the elevator began to move.

That last exchange between Bozinov and the man behind the desk indicated that he was being followed. He knew that the agency would take care of him. How they would do so he did not know.

The elevator stopped and Bozinov got out. Walking along the hall, he found his room number and inserted the electronic key that unlocked the latches. He went in, locking the door behind him. It was small and plain yet comfortable.

He set his bag on the table and, plopping it over, removed the bottom piece that held the legs, revealing a small device. He pulled the device out and activated it. This sensor would tell him if there were any bugs or any person other than himself inside the room. Although this was definitely a supposed safehouse, you never could be too sure, especially when there were other paying customers staying there.

The device beeped, signaling that everything was clear. Breathing a sigh of relief, he flopped down on the bed and fell asleep.

Greg the Hunter, as he was known, was not in the least bit happy when his colleague had informed him where he had followed Bozinov to the long-suspected safehouse for the Americans. They did not know how the public hotel worked, but they'd had enough people slip through their fingers to be suspicious. He pulled his car down the road and waited. He did not go in for he knew that they might recognize him. They would also be suspicious of anyone coming in after Bozinov.

It started to rain. He pulled his gun out of his coat and set it on the seat behind him in case any street people decided that his car would make a nice shelter. He figured that Bozinov would be making his plans while inside. He opened the bag beside him that revealed a computer terminal. Activating the communication device, he talked to his agency, instructing them to switch on the listening devices inside the building.

The devices were experimental and so would not be subject to any detection devices. They had been saving them for just this special occasion.

The man behind the front desk had been in the business for quite some time. When he had realized who it was that checked into the hotel, he knew something big was up because Bozinov would never take such a risk as leaving Moscow to contact someone; he would have used the television trick. He knew that when Bozinov replied "it is more occupied than you think" it meant there was trouble.

So bringing his communication device online, he decided to go to text mode so that no sound between him and the agency would be heard. He decided that it would be best to have the man tailing Bozinov tailed.

Chapter 9

November 27, 2071

Harrison awoke suddenly to the alarm. He leaned over and hit the clock, but for some reason it would not stop beeping. It wasn't until he had almost beaten the thing to death that he realized that the noise was not coming from the clock but from his computer terminal.

He set the clock back up on the table and, scrambling out of bed, made his way over to the dresser and brought the message up. "And I thought it was going to be another boring day," he said sarcastically.

The noise had waked him up at 1:30 a.m. and he had actually managed to get three hours of sleep. That was better than normal. At least for the life of a spy. *I've got to talk to my recruiter about these lousy hours*, he thought.

The message came up on the screen. It was text only, no voice or picture. *Must be pretty damn important*, he thought. He studied the words realizing that it was big. Bigger than he had seen in a long time.

His brow was low, for he was deeply disturbed. Turning the computer off, he sat down on the edge of the bed and thought. *If Bozinov was willing to blow his cover and go to a safehouse, something enormous is about to happen. And it appears from the guy shadowing him that they are on to him. I just wonder who else knows about this.*

Realizing that he was wasting precious time daydreaming, he got up and got into the shower. There was no telling when he would get the chance to take one again so he took an extra long one.

After having dried himself and putting his clothes on, he walked into the study. He then removed a row of encyclopedias from the one shelf to reveal a panel. Reaching in, he removed the panel and pulled out a suitcase. He unlocked the case to reveal a rather large gun. Looking at everything to verify he had all the pieces and checking to see if everything looked in working order, he then closed the case and walked over to the desk. He opened the drawer and grabbed a small handgun which he tucked inside of his coat. Grabbing his keys, he left the house, got into his car and set out to find Bozinov's shadow.

As Harrison drove along, he thought over and over again of the message that had appeared on his computer screen: *Bozinov at Riviera, being tailed. Follow and neutralize if necessary.*

Being tailed? he thought. *Being tailed by whom? What is Bozinov up to and what has the person tailing him learned?*

These were all questions that Harrison wanted answered. He was approaching the Riviera. It was just around the block. He pulled the car off to the side because he did not want to be recognized. He got out of the car and headed down the alley. There he found a man with a shopping cart and all his possessions. It was mostly garbage, cans and stuff, but it was all he had.

Taking out his wallet, he pulled out three hundred dollars to buy the cart and gave it to the man, who looked like he had just won the lotto, and told him to get lost. Now his disguise was complete.

He pushed the cart out of the alley and proceeded to walk up the street. He played the part well, looking in cans and talking to himself so that people thought he was drunk. He made his way slowly but surely toward the Riviera.

As he got closer, he realized that it would be foolish to purposely avoid looking at the individual in the car since everyone else was pestering him, so he decided to make a good show of it.

Walking up to the window, he knocked on the glass. "Hey, man that's a nice ride, you help me out," he said, letting out a rather disgusting belch.

The man shadowing Bozinov looked thoroughly disgusted. "Get out here!" he shouted, waving his arms to fend off any other would-be peddlers. He then flung his cigarette butt at them.

This started a real frenzy because all the peddlers realized that there was still a little bit left of the cigarette and they all began tackling one another for it. Harrison, using the commotion, slipped quietly into the nearby alley and used an old garbage can to hide behind, while still being able to see what was going on.

He rummaged into the shopping cart where he had put his case, opened it and took out a small listening device and aimed it at the car while the other part went into his ear. At first he heard static and then....

"Yes, General, there has been no movement since Bozinov went inside."

That must be the man inside the car, Harrison thought.

"Bah! This is preposterous. We have all we need now. There is no use for this constant waste of time. This will give us Bozinov and all his co-conspirators," said another voice from somewhere. It was a transmission of some sort. "Apprehend them all, call all the backup you need and I want Bozinov alive. Is that understood?" the voice said.

"Yes sir, General Polov," he said.

At that, the transmission ended. *So*, Harrison thought, *it is Polov who is behind all of this.* Harrison took the earpiece out of his ear and, reaching into his shopping cart, pulled out a trunk. He opened it up to reveal a small computer which he quickly brought online. There was no point in being secretive about how he sent the message to the safehouse, for he did not know how much time he had. Bringing out the small handheld dish that would allow a satellite link-up, he quickly got online with the website and sent a message directly to the computer terminal in the safehouse.

The clerk at the desk was wiping down the bench with a furniture wax. It was old and yet its finish was like new. It had been built over two hundred years ago, and even though it was not his, everyone that worked for the agency at the safehouse took great care of it. As he wiped, he let his mind wonder and his thoughts drift, for this, although it was work, was the most un-stressful thing he could think to do.

His terminal beeped with an incoming message. *Strange*, he thought, *it is not coded.* He stopped what he was doing to hit the key to receive the message. And there across the screen was the message that he knew would one day come.

They are coming to take the safehouse by force. Bozinov is the reason.

Without hesitation, he moved the books off of the bookshelf to reveal a red button which he then pressed. The light in the corner turned red and a bell began to ring. Two attendants quickly came to him, whom he instructed to move Bozinov quickly and prepare to repel an attack.

Bozinov had just sat down in the chair when the bell began to ring. It was sounding all over the building. The door burst open and two men came rushing in and grabbed Bozinov.

"What's going on?" he demanded.

"We are being taken down," said one of the men. "We have orders to get you safely out of here and out to the United States. Now let's go." Half escorting, half shoving Bozinov through the door, they grabbed his belongings and ran down the hallway to the service elevator. They got inside and headed for the basement.

Bozinov took this opportunity to put his coat on and put some of his other belongings in his suitcase. The door opened and all over the place were various weapons. The one man armed himself with all the heavy weapons and the other with as many handguns as he could. They then gave Bozinov a pistol. "Do you know how to use one of these?" he asked.

"Yes," Bozinov replied.

"Good. Don't unless you absolutely have to," the one man said.

They led Bozinov down a chamber until they reached a sewer cover. Grabbing a crowbar, the men began to pry off the cover. Bozinov was waiting for the stench to reach up and grab his very soul, but it didn't. Instead, as they all climbed down, one switched on a light to reveal a tunnel that was perfectly clean.

"This isn't a sewer?"

"No," replied the one man, "but it looks like one from everyone's perspective outside."

Taking Bozinov by the arm, they quickly fled down the corridor.

Meanwhile, the forces arrived. The Hunter saluted the chief of the police forces.

"Sergeant, that is your objective," to which he pointed to that house. "Nobody gets out. Is that understood?"

"Yes, sir," he replied.

"I want Bozinov alive. Under no circumstance is he to be killed," he said. "Do I make myself clear to you?" he said as he shook his finger in the sergeant's face.

"Yes, sir," the other replied stiffly. "One thing, sir, what do we do about any others?"

The Hunter looked at him for a long moment, and then with a look of contempt for life, he replied, "Cut them to pieces," and with that he walked away.

The clerk, now carrying a weapon and full body armor, walked one last time behind his desk to look at the beautiful wood. He loved that piece of furniture. It was the only thing of beauty that he ever got to appreciate, and now it would be gone. He looked at himself in the reflection of the finish on the table and wondered if he was making a difference in the world at all.

He then came back from his reflection into his life and, moving some more of the books off the shelf, revealed a small key which he promptly grabbed and squeezed tightly into his hand.

Chapter 10

"All the barricades are in position, all the spies have been taken out of the building through the tunnels and the lift gates are ready to go," said one of the hotel people.

"Good work, although looking at that force outside, I doubt it will be enough," said the clerk. Picking up a microphone, he made an announcement throughout the building. "Attention, attention, before the assault begins, I want to stress to each and every one of you the need to maintain their position. There will be no retreat, no pulling out. We make our stand here. If by some way we are able to successfully repel the enemy, we will begin an evacuation through the tunnels. Do not lose hope! Remember that any sacrifice that is made here only helps the world to be a better place. We must give our operatives as much time between us and them, so we need to hold this building as long as we can. Good luck to everyone." At that he put the microphone down.

He looked at the man standing next to him and nodded for them to begin.

The sergeant was readying his men when from windows in the building and from holes in the walls came a spray of bullets. They caught a few men in transition and some lazy or sloppy people off guard. It was no consequence to the sergeant for he figured they were useless anyway. From behind the barricade, he radioed his battering team to begin the assault.

It was a noble attempt but a pretty futile one. There was no way the resistance fighters could stop the assault. They were not getting through the armored vehicles that were acting like barricades for the troops.

The people were not prepared for the assault that was about to befall them for they figured that they would want them alive. The assault was no more then grenade guns aimed at the front wall of the building, but they were very effective at bringing down the whole side of the building at once.

The sergeant gave the order to fire and grenades were thrown at the front of the building to blow large holes that the men could run through. Then guns fired simultaneously at the front of the building. The explosion ripped through the front wall as cries went out from the men and women as they were ripped apart from the debris spray. Bodies and limbs went flying in all directions as the sounds made any standing there instantly deaf.

Then came the barrage of bullets that finished off anyone that might have survived the onslaught. The clerk slid his way down the stairs, having been hit several times. The troops began to pour in and an occasional battle of gun shots went on throughout the house until there was nothing but silence.

The clerk, having been fatally wounded, found himself alone downstairs. It was only a matter of time before they came down and found him, so he had to hurry.

He tried to walk to the panel on the far wall, but stumbled and fell. He cringed in pain as the floor seemed to hit all the areas that he had been shot. His breathing was difficult, for one of his lungs had collapsed and he was coughing up blood.

Somehow though, he managed to get his arms up so that he might pull himself along. He managed to make it to the wall. There he had to stop, for his head had gotten light from the lack of blood in his body. He felt he might pass out, but he shook himself to try to shrug it off one last time. Pulling himself up, he tore at a part of the wall to reveal a secret panel. Opening the panel, there were two buttons and a key hole.

Still grasping the key tightly in his hand, he looked at it, and then slowly put it into the key hole and turned. As he did this the panel seemed to come to life with blinking lights and warning signs. He then lifted, with all of his strength, both of his arms and pushed the two buttons.

The man tailing Bozinov had been watching the battle from outside when the blast came. He had wanted to be safe while the troops took care of these matters. His job was not to be a man who just ran blindly into a room, shooting at everything that moved like a mindless zombie. Rather, his job was much more personal. He would find out who was in the room and know everything about them before he ran into the room shooting at everything that moved.

The Hunter was knocked onto his back all the way into the beginning of the alley when the explosion blew. It engulfed the entire building, including the two buildings beside it. The flames licked up anyone standing in the street, vaporizing them in an instant. Those that were hiding in something were killed by the sheer heat alone or the lack of oxygen that the fire took. Shrapnel was falling from the sky like missiles, intent on hitting anyone that the explosion missed.

The man quickly crawled himself behind a couple of cans to protect himself. He needed backup, he needed a plan, he needed something. He just did not know what to do at that moment. The thought that they would all commit suicide had never occurred to him. They had already risked to much to let it go. Pulling out a portable communicator, he called into his office.

The explosion was over. Only what was left of the buildings and several cars were on fire. There were fire trucks and people running about to and fro, shouting and yelling. There were crowds of people around watching. Some of the street walkers had gotten rowdy, trying to·steal just about anything they could get their hands on. They were being pursued and taken to jail by the local police. There were fire hoses crisscrossing in between the fire trucks and what was left of the cars.

More of the Hunter's men arrived, some in military uniforms. They began to sweep the street of anybody getting in the way. They all reported to him and he gave them their orders as he always did, but he was seriously trying not to be nauseous. Eventually he leaned up against a wall, sank down to his feet and hung his head in failure.

Polov sighed. The news of Bozinov's demise had come and he was not happy about it. He had wanted to take personal charge in being the one who interrogated him. He would enjoy it. He always had a desire to watch a man's defenses break down bit by bit until he was begging to tell you information. He would read about it in history, the things they did during WWII in Germany.

He used to go down to the interrogation center and watch the games, as he called it. He would watch the emotion their eyes, he could tell when they were experiencing pain and what they did to control it. It was important they he know what torture did to a man, so he could master its use one day. Now his day would not come.

He expressed his displeasure to the Hunter. Although he hammered him pretty hard, he did not let him have it to much. The end result was the same, and the Hunter was a good man, he needed his loyalty. Nothing was leaked, so he could carry out his plan.

He fantasized about being a national hero to the state. His picture on the front page of the papers. He would make promises to the people, show how he is working for them, and when the war was over seize power and bring about a new world.

They would think him mad if they knew all about him. Yet history repeatedly showed that every madman was fully supported while he was winning. He would only be labeled a madman if he did not succeed.

He sighed again. "Oh well," he said aloud. It was still a victory nonetheless. Bozinov's companions were dead, Bozinov was dead. Everything could proceed as planned. He could expose Bozinov now as a traitor. He could carry out his plan as before. It was just he had been looking so much forward to the interrogation. He sighed. *Such is war*, he thought.

Chapter 11

The fire had been reduced to smoldering ashes. The Hunter and three others were picking their way through the blackened rubble. He stopped and put his foot up on what was left of a wall. He looked around. There was nothing but scorched earth and ruin. The men had established a far perimeter around the area to keep the general populace out.

The Hunter dispatched the fire trucks back to their stations, although most of them were gone anyway. Only the Hunter, his men and some smoke and ashes were left.

He shook his head. He just could not believe it. They had taken everybody out. They were all dead, their men, his men. Only himself, the sergeant and two others had survived. He let out a big sigh.

He was about to pack up and leave. There was no use for him to stay. Oh, they would go through the usual forensics, but the sergeant could handle that. Then suddenly a call came out.

"Sir, you had better come see this," one of the men said. The man was bent over and pointing down.

The Hunter thought maybe he had found Bozinov's body, although it couldn't amount to much.

He walked over to the area that the man was pointing to and as he got closer he could see some light coming out from underneath the boards. He moved quickly to where the other man was at. He stopped short as he realized what he was seeing. *Oh no*, he thought.

"Clear those boards," he commanded the man, as if somehow what he was seeing was not actually there. With his mouth open and his head spinning, he looked down the long well-lit tunnel.

The Hunter quickly gathered his thoughts. "Sergeant, are any of the bodies found Bozinov's?"

"No, sir. However, a full investigation into all the debris to discover...."

"Yes, yes," he said, waving his hand and cutting him off in midsentence "You run your investigation." *Policemen always were like a bunch of dumb buffoons*, he thought. It was obvious that Bozinov had escaped, because if they had the tunnel they could have all escaped, and the number that had died wouldn't have had to sacrifice themselves so needlessly. They knew that we were going to take the building; they had stayed behind to buy him time to escape.

"Sergeant, I want two armed men down that tunnel in pursuit and I want three of your men. Two of them in one car, the other with me."

"Yes, sir," he replied as he waved at a group of his officers toward him.

He instructed the few that were to go down the tunnel to be quick in their movement because he wanted them to intercept Bozinov before he got out—wherever that was.

Although, he knew at that point, now hours later, they were long gone. Quickly climbing down the ladder, they ran off down the tunnel.

The other three remained standing there, waiting for instructions. The Hunter motioned to them and told two of them to get in their car and the other to get into his car. All of them were armed to the hilt.

Polov had begun to wish he had not gotten out of bed when the word on Bozinov came. Now he knew he should not have.

Polov was holding his head in his hands and rubbing the bridge of his nose when he angrily snapped at the terminal and the Hunter's face. "You mean you let them get away!"

"Sir, uh...yes, sir."

Polov's face softened a bit and took on a look of empathy. "You know, you are my most trusted agent. You are the one I call when I need someone I can count on. You are the best, which is why I wanted you specifically on this assignment." Polov sighed. "But you are disappointing me now. This report it is the kind I would expect from…a policeman."

This, of course, was a great insult to the Hunter and Polov knew it. He would not insult the man further, but like all good leaders, he knew how to bring out the best in his subordinates, if he pushed the right buttons.

The Hunter kept his face stoic, but inside he was seething. He had never been called a policeman, which denoted that he was just another imbecile. He was rather troubled though that Polov would say such a thing to him, after all his years of service. *There must be more riding on this than anything I have ever encountered*, he thought.

"I cannot express to you the importance of Bozinov being stopped. The price of failure for you, for me and for a great deal others will be incredibly great. But enough said, you still have my confidence, which is why I want you to continue the pursuit. Now if you would be so kind as to please kill Mr. Bozinov, I am going to have my afternoon tea, where I will await your report of good news." With that the screen went blank.

"I'll tell you what you can do with your tea," the Hunter muttered under his breath.

Packing up his gear, the Hunter and the officer got into the car. The Hunter pulled out his briefcase. The officer became curious and wanted to know what the Hunter was doing.

The Hunter said, "I am going to find out where that tunnel goes. That tunnel was broad and was cut by some sort of machinery. There is no way they could have mounted such an operation without us knowing about it. So I am going to go online and find out when it was built and where it goes."

The Hunter called up the net, and accessing city hall, he began to dig. He went back further and further, giving the computer keywords to aid it in its search. The computer then brought up a magazine article entitled, "The Tunnels of WWII." He read it and it talked about how they had dug tunnels underground deep enough to be a shelter against bomb attacks, but would allow the civilians to get from one place to another without fear of being harmed. That was what gave him the clue.

Accessing the city's blueprints, he brought up WWII tunnels. The computer then showed him a map of the city's many tunnels. He found his location and there it was. He quickly found out where it led, and yelling out the window at the other two to follow quickly, he shoved the computer aside and raced down the road. The hunt was on again.

Chapter 12

The three men raced down the tunnel. It was not a long way, only about three miles, but Bozinov was an older man and not conditioned for it. When they had run nearly two miles straight without let up, he began to breath really heavily, coming in gasps. He begun to clutch at his side as he stumbled along. Finally, he slumped to the floor, nearly passing out.

The other two saw him and raced back to him to see if he was okay. Kneeling down beside him, the one man pulled out a handkerchief and wiped his brow. "You are out of shape there, comrade."

Bozinov tried to muster a smile. In between his breaths, he said, "I'm only a few days from retirement you know. This game is for you young guys. I'm too old for this sort of thing."

The man smiled and pulled out a flask filed with water. He gave it to Bozinov, who gulped it down quickly. Color began to return to his face. Although he still looked like he was in desperate need of a nap.

"We must be going again. We have lost precious time already. There is a car waiting for us."

"Does it have air conditioning?" Bozinov asked.

The man chuckled. "Yes, it has air conditioning. This ain't no backyard operation. We may be covert, but we do things in style."

Bozinov grinned and got up, only the pace was slowed down to a half jog.

They still moved quickly though. Occasionally they stopped down to a walking pace, and then got back up to their run speed. Finally, they came to the end. It was a ladder.

Bozinov looked up his head swooned. His heart was pounding. *Too many fried foods*, he thought. He groaned and leaned against the ladder, resting his head against the cool metal. It felt good.

"Come on," they urged him, "quickly now! You can rest later." They started shoving at him as he began to climb.

It seemed like an eternity. And yet all the while his thoughts kept going through his mind, telling him to stop, rest and relax, but he kept climbing. He never looked up and never looked down. He just kept climbing hand over hand.

He nearly bumped his head on the manhole cover before he realized that he had reached the surface. Reaching up, he began to push it out of the way.

The car was up there waiting for them. Bozinov pulled himself up and the other two men quickly got out of the tunnel and into the car. They shoved Bozinov into the back with one of the men and the other drove. They tore down the street, anxious to get out from the city.

The Hunter and the others raced down the streets until there was some jam-up. They came screeching to a halt. Apparently something had happened with a couple of cars and a bunch of street people. Honking his horn, he began shouting. "Get out of the way! Police business!"

One of the people involved stopped his discussion to look at them and then very emphatically gave them the middle finger. Another person threw a rock at the car.

The officer in the car was about to get out to try and break it up when the Hunter said, "Never mind!" and reaching behind the seat, pulled out an automatic weapon. Getting out of the car, he began to fire it up in the air.

The people moved quickly out of the way, yelling and screaming as they thought they would be killed. They were not too far off in their assessment had they not moved out of his way.

Jumping in the car, the officer began to yell at him about it being a civilian neighborhood and what he was doing.

"Shut up!" he said and threw the car into gear, plowing into the cars in front of him and pushing them out of the way.

Bozinov's vehicle moved quickly down the side streets. It was a bumpy ride and none to comfortable as he was being forced to keep his head down by the other operatives. His neck began to ache.

However, he did not need to worry about his neck anymore when the car came to a screeching turn, throwing Bozinov over the seat and into the front. They had just barely avoiding a broadside collision with a cop car. It was the Hunter.

The Hunter quickly swerved to the left, avoiding being hit in the side as Bozinov's car almost sideswiped him. Quickly, he put the car in reverse, and backing up, he threw the car in drive and sped off after Bozinov.

They caught up to them quickly. Bozinov had scrunched himself down onto the floor in the front. The one man was driving and the other was in the back seat.

The man in the back seat pulled out his automatic weapon, and using it to break the back window glass, let fly a nonstop spray of bullets.

The Hunter was yelling into the terminal about getting a helicopter when the spray of bullets came blasting through the windshield. There was a quick bend to the right, however, and ducking down from the bullets, he swerved to the left, missing the turn and plowing into a storefront. The other car behind them made the turn. Cursing and swearing, he backed out and pursued.

The other cars were exchanging automatic weapon fire as they sped down the street. They were weaving in and out of traffic as they exchanged gunfire. They turned down a side street and hit an unsuspecting pedestrian along the way. The woman flew up across the car before being sprawled upon the pavement, dead. The cars never even stopped. Other observers, horrified at what they had just seen, realized their fate too if they did not quickly move, and fought to get out of the way of the cars and the bullets.

Bozinov's driver quickly cut up onto the sidewalk, knocking down signs and anything that might be in his way, with the other cars following suit. As they reached the end of the road, instead of making the turn, they cut into an open field, across the grass and onto another street.

The officer in the Hunter's car had had enough. They had already killed one woman in the chase; he wasn't going to see any more get killed. The whole chase was out of line and he would see to it that the Hunter and his goons would be brought up on charges. The idea was to keep the peace not subvert it.

"Give me that automatic weapon," the Hunter said to the officer.

"No!" he replied angrily. This was it, he'd had enough. Taking the weapon in hand, he aimed it at the Hunter. "You are under arrest as are the officers in front of us. This is a residential area, you can't go shooting it up. For god sakes, man, we hit someone back there and you did not even stop! So I am giving you a direct order now. Stop the car, stop the car this minute!"

The Hunter made no effort to stop despite the gun barrel pointing at him from the officer. Instead, he just grinned. "If you are not going to help, then you should take a nap," the Hunter said smugly.

The Hunter, reaching with his left hand, grabbed a gun from his side, crossed his body with it and shot the officer in the seat beside him, killing him. He then took the weapon from the dead officer's hand.

"Glad you saw it my way," he said.

Harrison had been watching the blip on his screen, for he had bugged the Hunter's vehicle. He saw them all speed off, and by the erratic turns, he knew there was a chase going on. *I've seen enough*, he decided. It was time to take care of business. Shoving his stuff aside, he raced down the street to his car.

The spray of gunfire continued between the two cars. Bozinov's car cut through a gas station, smashing into a car as they went through. The car spun around, knocking the pumps all over as an enormous explosion went up, sending an umbrella-shaped fire cloud expanding in all directions.

The police car was too late to swerve. It went right through the cloud as the men screamed in terror, but they managed to come out unscathed. The fire, however, had engulfed the rest of the station, sending torches of intense heat and flame in all directions. The Hunter stopped. There was no way he could go through. Pulling the car up to the corner, he went around.

Harrison watched the exchange from a nearby overpass. He stopped his car to examine the route that was being taken. He realized that the route would circle back around to a nearby road. Harrison jumped in his car and sped off in the direction of that route. He wanted to get there in time to take the nearest car out at least. He quickly drove down the road. He got to the junction where they would meet. He quickly checked his scope and sure enough they were heading right for him. He got out of the car and opened the trunk.

Inside the trunk was a shoulder-mounted rocket gun. He set up the gun and programmed it so that when he had a target lock it would follow that target until the target was destroyed.

Closing the trunk, he moved quickly behind a wall so that he would not be seen and so they would be coming right at him. He wanted to hit the car from head on, that way the car behind it would think that the rocket had come from Bozinov. He needed to keep his cover so he could take out that next car.

The cars came over the hill; Bozinov's was a little ahead. Mounting the rocket, he waited for the next vehicle. It came over the hill. *Wait*, he thought. He locked the target with the guidance system. As Bozinov's car came flying by, he squeezed the trigger, letting the rocket fire.

The missile shot straight out and hit the car dead on. The missile impact shot through the car from one end to the other, causing explosion and fire in its wake. The sides of the car literally blew off in a thousand directions.

The Hunter slammed his brakes, bringing his car to a screeching halt. Overwhelmed at the firepower that Bozinov obviously possessed, he quickly got back on the terminal to ask where his helicopter was. He was going to have to hang back a bit so that the same fate did not befall him. It turned out that it was good he had gotten a little behind from the gas station incident. For if he hadn't, he would have surely been caught up in the missile attack.

The car in front of him had become a tower of flame and flying shrapnel. The vehicle was still moving as it swerved off the path and smashed into another car, catching it on fire.

Upset and his ego a bit bruised, the Hunter began beating on his steering wheel, cursing. He shoved the car into gear and waded through the wreckage. Once again the pursuit was on.

"Whoa!" Bozinov said. He had thought the rocket had launched from them. "That was awesome! Good work!" He slapped the guy in the back seat on the shoulder. He did not realize that they carried that kind of firepower.

However, the driver was quick to correct him. "That missile shot did not come from us!" he yelled at Bozinov.

"What!" he said back to the driver. "What are you saying?" he cried.

The driver, still bent on driving like a madman, was trying to talk and concentrate at the same time. Looking over at his shoulder at Bozinov, he said, "Normally we might have a few special surprises for them, but we were not prepared for this one. We never had the time to load the car with that kind of firepower. Even if we had, it would be riding around in the trunk. It seems there is someone else out there that knows about you. Let's just hope they were aiming for that car and not for us."

Bozinov turned back around toward the man in the back seat. He was in a daze. He did not know how everything had managed to fall apart around him. He quickly snapped out of it, getting back to the task at hand. "Hey," he said to the man in the back seat.

The man did not move. Bozinov's eyes went wide. "Hey," he said, pulling on the man by the arm. Turning him over, he saw that the man was dead. A bullet had hit him square in the forehead. "He's dead!" he yelled back to the man driving.

Harrison quickly got his composure and, throwing the rocket launcher back into the car, dived into the car. He needed to get ahead of the second car if he was to take it out as well.

He knew that the other car was going to have to take a few moments before it could give chase again, but he was too close and it would take him a moment to get the rocket launcher ready again.

He drove off in the direction of Bozinov. They were beginning to get in more wooded areas now and he began going up more and more mountainous terrain. The one side of the road was actually a cliff that dropped off to quite a depth below.

As he got to the top of an expanse, he decided it is where he would make his stand. It was an excellent spot. Both sides of the road could be seen. The direction of Bozinov went off into a valley, where he could actually see Bozinov's car moving. The other was the direction the second car would come from.

There was cover too. There was a rather large weeping willow that would afford him the cover necessary to complete his task. Quickly getting out of the car, he set to work. He pulled the launcher out from the seat beside him. He set it down and, moving to the back of the car, quickly opened the trunk and pulled out a large case. Taking it over to the launcher, he set it down as well. Opening it, he grabbed the last rocket. "I better not miss," he mused.

He loaded the weapon and set his program again. It would once again follow a target that had been radar locked until it struck. He settled himself down by the tree. He could see Bozinov's car in the distance. Turning the other direction, he waited for the other car that had the Hunter. *Wait for it*, he thought as he looked for his target.

The noise began to ring in Harrison's ears. It was a sound that began to get louder and louder, a pulsating sound that seemed to come from all around him at once. He let the rocket destined for the Hunter droop towards the ground. The sound was almost on top of him now. It was a sound that sent chills through him, for it meant only one thing: a helicopter.

Its size was massive as it came up across the top of the cliff. Going right over him, it blocked out the sun. Harrison dove towards the trunk of the tree hoping that those in the helicopter would not notice him. He could tell from first sight that it was no ordinary copter. It was a military one. It held all types of firepower and he would be an easy target.

The helicopter flew right overhead and passed him, heading in the direction of Bozinov. He knew it was going to target Bozinov's car. It was hanging low and was no doubt waiting for him. He looked down the road at the approaching vehicle. He then looked back at the helicopter. He had only one shot. Glancing at the rocket he held, he made his decision.

Turning around and standing up now to give him a better sight, he aimed at the helicopter. The radar quickly locked its target. He fired.

Onboard the helicopter, a red light signaled. "We've been radar locked!" one man yelled to the pilot.

The pilot shoved the stick down into a bank shot, a desperate and daring maneuver. However, it was to no avail. The missile found its intended target.

It was not a clean hit, but it was good enough. Hitting the rear tail, it blew off the rear of the helicopter. It hurtled downward in a spiraling ball of flame, where it crashed in a large wooded area, catching the trees and surrounding bush on fire.

Harrison was pleased with himself but quickly recovered as he dove back by the tree. He had become keenly aware of the approaching vehicle from behind. The second car sped past him with no mind. Once again he had not been noticed and he let out an exhaustive sigh. Now he would have to follow the Hunter and hope a gun would be enough.

The Hunter, for his part, had not seen the exchange of firepower, for he was on the other side of the mountain at the time. He drove past the place where he could see the smoke and flames coming out from behind the trees but paid it no mind.

I wonder where my helicopter is, he thought. "You want a job done…" he said exasperatingly and continued to gain on the other vehicle.

"Stay down," the driver told him. "We aren't out of this yet." He kept his composure, but unknown to Bozinov he was .

clutching his side. He had been hit. His head began to swoon as the blood pulsed out of his side.

"You're going to have to make a break for it. I'm going to stop and you get out and run. You know the way to go from here."

"What about you?" Bozinov asked.

"Never mind about me. I can take care of myself," he snapped, trying to control the car as he began to go off of the road.

"Just get that information to the free world!" he yelled at Bozinov.

The driver swerved the car into the park as they hit a tree, bringing the car to a sudden and none-to-pleasant halt. Bozinov was dazed from the impact, but turning to his compatriot, he found the man slumped over the wheel. Believing the driver to be dead, he jumped out of the car and ran.

The driver wasn't dead though. He began to come to just in time to see Bozinov running off in the distance. He smiled, for he had done his job. He looked down at his wound and saw that it was too late. He wished that he had never come to. It would have been better had he never woken up again.

He eventually heard the noise of a car, whose engine was racing. Hearing the screech of tires, he saw the pursuant coming to a halt nearby. He had done his duty. It was what he had been trained for, what he believed in, and now there was only one last duty to perform. He picked up the gun next to him and put it to his head....

Chapter 13

Bozinov was running when he heard a gunshot. He stopped and, crouching low, looked fearfully around him. When he did not see anything, he continued his run.

He was running scared. He was not thinking. The only thing he could hear in his mind as it screamed at him was escape. He thought of his beloved. His heart was pounding in his chest. He was running into all sorts of things, until he practically ran straight into a large bush. The impact propelled him over the top where he landed with a large thud. The bush made a large cracking sound as its trunk was broken by Bozinov's onslaught.

Bozinov got quickly to his feet and continued his run, hoping that no one saw him or heard him.

The Hunter did not see, but he heard. Looking up from the dead man, he ran full speed in the direction of the sound.

Bozinov was clutching at his side as his breathing once more came in gasps. He tripped and fell. The gun came flopping out of his hand and, bouncing across the ground, fell into a hole such like a rabbit makes. Realizing quickly what had happened, he scrambled up and frantically tore at the hole's opening, but to no avail, the gun was lost.

He heard an approaching rustling; it was his pursuant. He turned from the direction of the sound and fled.

His heart was still pounding; he could hear the sound behind him.

His head began to swim and he gasped for breath as he ascended a small hill. There was no brush at that point. He was in full open ground. *I have to cover this quickly*, he thought.

It was not a really large hill; however, with his breathing already coming in gasps, and his strength drained, it seemed like a mountain.

The Hunter moved with the speed and agility of an Olympian. He never gave up, and he never got tired. That was why they called him the Hunter. He would stalk you until he wore you down and then he would get you. He could sense his prey, much like an animal that could smell the prey long before it could see it. He became absorbed by him. It was as if he could see the person running, trying to flee from him. He would anticipate everything now. There would be no more mistakes. He would win.

The Hunter, though, was still unaware of the person shadowing him. His one weakness: he would focus on the target to the exclusion of all others.

Harrison had pulled up in his car. After assessing the situation, he got out his binoculars. He adjusted the magnification as the computer adjusted the focus. He spotted them. Bozinov had gone in an almost complete circle. He was stumbling up a nearby ridge. He estimated the top of the hill to be about three hundred yards. Moving quickly and efficiently, he pulled out his laser-sighted rifle.

Bozinov was now nearing the top. He grasped at the ground as he lost his footing and slid down a few feet. Clawing at the ground, his hand bleeding, he stopped his downward motion and pulled himself up as he once again began his ascent. He glanced down to see the Hunter coming up the hill. Frantic, his heart and mind racing, he propelled himself forward.

He was cresting the ridge as a pain ripped through him like none other he had ever experienced. His heart pounding, his vision blurred and unable to breathe, he fell to the ground.

Harrison saw Bozinov go over the ridge as his pursuant came into his view. Slowly and with a steady hand, he sighted his target and brought the laser point onto him.

The Hunter was grinning as he got to the top of the hill. He was unaware of the small red dot that had appeared upon his back, where the laser sight of Harrison's gun had found its target. He saw Bozinov. *I have won, I have won,* he thought.

Harrison squeezed the trigger. The single shot ripped through the Hunter's body, knocking him back as he tumbled toward the side of the hill where there was a ridge.

His thoughts were locked in a state of repeat, like a record that had developed a scratch. *He won*, he thought, as he fell. *He won.* He thought no more.

Harrison let out a deep sigh of relief. Shouldering the rifle, he began the trek in the direction of the man he had felled. He was glad it was over, for now Bozinov was free to get his secrets to the world that he so much believed in. He walked along the side of the hill, coming up to the man he had felled. He searched his body and took the gun from his hand.

He then began to scale the hill to see if he could catch a glimpse of Bozinov running off into the sunset. *I am going to have a lot of reports to fill out when I get back to my office,* he thought. He sighed. He hated paperwork.

He got up to the hilltop and stopped short. With a look of surprise and horror, he saw Bozinov lying there, breathing very raspy and clutching his chest. He ran quickly to the man.

He quickly told him to relax. He was an agent working on his side and he was there to help. Removing the man's coat, he looked at him quickly but could find no bullet wounds on him.

Bozinov was clutching at his chest as waves of pain ripped over him. He was having a heart attack. There was nothing Harrison could do.

Then, in a brief moment of relapse, Bozinov spoke to him. "Invasion, Canada," was all he could muster at the moment.

He was holding tightly around Harrison's arm as if he were falling, clutching onto a single branch for dear life. Gasping for air, his voice came softly now. Harrison bent over him to hear. "The queen...freighter. Tell the shipmaster Bozinov alpha 1 beta Charlie go US."

His hand went limp and his head rolled back. He saw in his mind the woman he loved. She was all he wanted. Now his dream was over and he would never see her. His eyes closed. Darkness enclosed his spirit.

Harrison lay him back on the ground. He said a silent prayer over the man. He was not a religious person, but he felt a certain kinship to him.

After standing up, he set out in the direction of the sunset. His destiny lay west on another continent. His country, his home and the people he sought to protect. His paperwork was going to have to wait.

Chapter 14

Doug knocked on the door as Pam yelled out, "Just a minute!" She put the baby in the playpen and went to open the door.

"Hi," she said, greeting him. She opened the door wider and gestured for him to come in.

He walked into her room and pulled off his coat, setting it in the plush chair that looked rather inviting for him after the long hours he had spent in the lab.

"How's he doing?" he asked.

"Oh, he's great. Me, I'm tired!"

Doug laughed. He knew nothing about children other than having watched Pam for some time, but he was starting to realize how much work they were. "Well, maybe we can tire him out a bit," he replied.

Doug got down on the floor with the child and began to make funny faces at him. The child responded with a fit of laughter. Doug in turn began to get more and more silly as Pam watched, taking in all the wonderful excitement. "I wish I had a camera right now! You have no idea how much all this is really worth, if I don't tape it and show it to the people at work. Let me see, Dr. McDowell, just how much money should I blackmail you with?" she said laughingly.

Doug smiled at her. "Probably more than I could afford," he replied. The baby was bouncing his hands up and down and making all kinds of squeaking noises.

"He is such a happy child," Pam said, smiling.

"Yes, he is," he replied, lifting the baby up over his head and down on his back, holding him by his feet while he hung upside down.

The child was laughing the whole time as Doug basically roughhoused with him. Pam watched the two of them going on and begun to wonder to herself. *You know he would make a good father*, she thought. *We've been together now quite a long time.*

I remember the first time we met. He was a dashing, hotshot scientist. It was my first day and when I walked into the lab for the first time, I walked right into him, spilling his coffee all over his suit. I was so sorry, I started to cry. He must have felt bad for me because he took my hands and told me that it was okay. He was on his way out and there was no real harm done. He smiled and I dried my tears and he introduced himself. He asked my name and I stuttered over it as he grinned. He told me he was looking forward to working together and that he would talk later. "Perhaps we could have lunch?" he asked. I was so stunned that my mouth actually hung open, at least until I snapped to it again and eagerly replied with a gasping yes!

As he walked out the door, he replied, "Great, but I don't recommend anything on the menu in this place!"

He made me laugh. It was incredible. He was so nice and kind. I realized it even more so when later I found out that he was on his way out to give a presentation to over four hundred delegates where he was the guest speaker. He never told me or complained to me about the coffee stain I gave him.

Pam came back to the present time, watching Doug and the child stacking blocks on the floor.

Doug was grinning ear to ear. "You know, some of this stuff is really neat. I think I enjoy playing with it more than the baby. It is fascinating, though, that some of the coolest gadgets he is not interested in. He would rather have a plastic spoon from the kitchen and use it to beat on anything that makes a drumming noise."

Pam had been watching the whole thing from behind clouded eyes and deep thought. *And now here we are today*, she thought. Her feelings were swelling in her. Like waves from oceans that come rolling upon the sand, so her feelings for Doug were.

"Amazing, isn't it?" said Pam. "Well, baby boy, Mommy is going to make your bottle."

The baby's face just lit up.

"He understood you!" said Doug, a little shocked.

"Of course he understood," Pam said, grinning at him. "I always say the same phrases for each thing. That way he understands what is going on. In time, he will say the same things back to me. That is how you teach a person both what you are trying to say and how to say it."

"Wow, what a great idea," Doug said

Pam rolled her eyes. *I still have to teach him a thing or two about children.*

She walked into the kitchen and opened the refrigerator and grabbed the special formula that Doug and Bill had made for her. She remembered the first time they gave it to him. She had to take it back to them and tell them to change it after the baby spit it out. She had tasted it herself and almost gagged. She was amazed that the child did not throw it up.

Doug and Bill were adamant about it though. They quoted tons of factual data. They were going on about nutrition and necessary chemistry and all that stuff. She just shook her head at both of them. She told them it tasted terrible, and if they could drink one bottle of it without gagging, she would drop the whole thing. Needless to say, after one gulp, Doug spit it across the room.

"I see your point," he said. He was struggling to find something to wash the taste out of his mouth. "What should we do?"

"Well, how about something that tastes like milk?" she said in a rather sarcastic tone. "Actually, if you can make it taste more like breast milk it would be better."

Doug and Bill looked at each other, then both looked at Pam. A couple of glances were made toward her chest, but were quickly diverted in some other direction.

Pam's cheeks turned a bit pink as she caught the glance. "Well, as long as it has some palatable taste anyway," she concluded and walked away.

Doug and Bill let out a sigh of relief.

She finished making the bottle and walked back in the room with Doug and the baby. Doug had the baby cradled in his arms.

Pam stopped short and just stared at him. All the rest of the room seemed to be a haze as a glow just emanated from the two of them. Doug looked up at her and their eyes met. They smiled at one another.

"Here, you want to feed him?" Pam asked.

"Uh, well, I ah…."

"Here, let me show you how." She gave him the bottle and helped him set the baby in a half-seated position.

The baby's arms started going all over the place as Doug just didn't seem to get it.

Pam, however, was able to put Doug's arms in the right position and was able to fix the situation. She then handed the bottle to Doug and showed him how to do it. "There you go," she said, brushing back her jet black hair and looking into the baby's face. She kissed him gently on the forehead like she always did. Although the baby was eating, he could see the look of love and approval that he had gotten from both of them and that was all he needed.

Doug smiled to himself and thought, *We definitely picked the right person for this.*

Pam took the baby into the other room, where she lay him down in the crib to go to bed. Tiptoeing out of the room, she shut the door and held one finger to her lips as she looked at Doug. Doug acknowledged the gesture with a nod and turned the baby monitor screen on. The picture came up on the screen in full color of what was going on in the room despite it being in total darkness.

Pam went about the kitchen and cleaned things up and then began to get some late-night dinner ready. She was feeling like a candlelit dinner.

Chapter 15

December 6, 2071

"Mr. President, CIA agent and head of national security to see you, sir."

"Show him in," the President said.

The President turned to look out of the Oval Office. He peered into the streets. There were fires from the cans of the street dwellers. There were so many homeless now, despite everything he as an elected official wanted to do. He had such dreams and such big plans.

Yet somehow when he got here, he too had been swept under by that political quagmire that had so many times stepped on his predecessors. He knew there was nothing he could do, there was nothing anyone could do now. He had failed. He had failed all those many people out there that huddled by the fires that burned against the bitter cold, the people huddling around them in an effort to keep at least some part of their bodies warm.

Every now and then, he could hear the goings-on from outside, despite the distance between him and the gate. Usually it was gunfire that the military was forced to fire off into the air to stop a situation from happening.

The military basically surrounded the White House permanently. It was to keep the outside crowds from overrunning the place. It was a sad day when America's own people would be placed under national security. The very foundation of the United States was for freedom. But what was he to do? He sighed.

The door opened and in stepped a CIA agent and a rather gruff-looking individual whose clothes were ragged. He looked as if he had not shaven, or taken a bath for that matter, in about a month. *Oh great, what have the outsiders done now?* he thought.

"Sir, this is one of our operatives from Europe, Harrison."

"It is an honor to meet you, sir," Harrison said while shaking the President's hand. "I must apologize for my attire. However, with the current situation, I felt it imperative that I speak with you right away."

The President motioned him to sit down in front of his desk as Harrison began to tell the tale of the imminent invasion through upper Canada. The President, a quiet man despite being a politician, just paced back and forth from wall to wall as Harrison's story unfolded before him.

When Harrison was finished, the President once again looked out the Oval Office window. He was staring at the outsiders wandering about, but he was a million miles away. Harrison fidgeted in his chair as if a little uncomfortable with the silence and the President's seemly calm manner.

Then, just before Harrison was about to attempt to clear his throat, the President snapped around and picked up a red phone on his desk. "Get me the general at NORAD, the joint chiefs and the Vice President. I want to hold an emergency conference now!"

Harrison was ordered to stay by the President, but was allowed to go and clean himself up. He was at least grateful for that. His rather haggard appearance was not all due to just a lack of bathing. His flight to get there had been one hellish experience.

After having left Bozinov, he moved as quickly as he could over the rough terrain back to his vehicle. Getting out the map, he located the nearest shipping ports and all the other surrounding ports. There were about fifty. He let out a big sigh. It was going to take awhile....

Subsequently, after much searching, Harrison finally came to the small port where the ship he sought was. He walked up and down the dock until he saw the freighter named the *Queen*. The dock was bustling with activity. Machinery was being used to load and unload crates and cargo on and off the ships. There were people moving about and vehicles going to and fro.

It did not look like a very safe place though. *Although safe is quite relative in today's world*, he thought. Nevertheless, the people around him looked like a bunch of cutthroats. He approached the gangplank of the one ship and started up it.

There was a sudden loud mechanical sound, one that he knew all too well. It was the sound of a gun being cocked. Stopping in the middle of the gangplank, he slowly turned around to see a rather gruff-looking Spaniard standing about twelve feet behind him with a shotgun pointed at him. He heard another sound in front of him this time. Looking in front of him, there was another one.

The one in front spoke to him. "Hey, hombre, you lost?"

This, of course, was a sarcastic jibe; he was going to be taken by these two regardless of what he said. Hopefully, he could reach through to them. *Well, here goes*, he thought.

"No, I need to speak with the shipmaster immediately! It is of the most serious of business. May I please speak with him?"

The one man seemed to ponder this for a moment, then nodding to the other man behind Harrison, he had him searched. The other man threw Harrison up against the side railing as he patted him down. He found an all-too-familiar bulge in the coat pocket of Harrison. He reached in and pulled out Harrison's handgun.

The Spaniard got in his face . His nose was practically touching Harrison's. "I thought you wanted to talk," he said.

"You never can be too careful," said Harrison as he grinned innocently. "Yes, I carry a gun, but I do need to talk to the shipmaster. It is urgent!"

The Spaniard backed up and said with a grin, "Yea, man, you gonna talk to him alright."

Motioning to the other man, they shoved him up the gangplank where the back of his head abruptly met the butt end of one of their rifles. He fell quickly to the deck where his ribs met the end of someone's foot as he was kicked. They gave him a full going over. This was intended to tenderize him, much like a piece of meat for chewing, but he blacked out from the many blows to his back, chest and face.

Harrison awoke to a bright light on him in a darkened room. He was sitting in a chair. Actually, he was tied to it, with his hands behind him. Dazed and sore, he became aware that he was still on the ship by the way it moved. They were moving! His stomach got queasy, partially because of the motion but mostly from the blows to his body. His senses gradually became aware of someone else in the room with him.

The man walked toward him. He stopped just short of coming into the light, although he could tell the man wore an all-white suit with a white shirt, white tie and white shoes.

"Why are you here, old boy?" said a sarcastic Englishman.

"Bozinov alpha 1 beta Charlie go US," was all he could muster to say.

The man's eyes closed until they became slits. Moving quickly towards Harrison, he grabbed the arms of the chair, bringing their faces within fractions of an inch.

"What do you know of Bozinov? Where is Bozinov?" the man asked with a hiss.

"Bozinov is dead. I am here in his place," Harrison said matter-of-factly.

The man eyed him coolly, then backing up, he grabbed a chair from a corner and moved into the lightened circle around Harrison. He pulled out a cigar and put it in his mouth and lit the end of it. He blew smoke in the direction of Harrison. The smell made him gag.

"I hope you don't mind if I smoke. It helps me to relax when I am agitated," he said with a look of a lion that had its prey trapped.

"Not at all," Harrison replied, shrugging to himself. *So I lied*, he thought. *Not that it will help me by not complaining.* He realized that escape was impossible. There was only so far one could go on a ship in the middle of the ocean. He could be hundreds of miles away from shore, which would make him shark food if he jumped. Although he might be shark food anyway with the way things were going.

The man puffed on his cigar for a while and then, looking at Harrison, said, "I'm still listening."

Harrison was relieved to see that the man would at least hear his tale before feeding him to the fish. So he began the long story of how he came to be on the ship.

Harrison's mind was snapped back to the present time when he almost walked straight into one of the guards that was to escort him. He had been pacing.

He was all clean and shaven now, although the soreness of his body was still with him. A constant reminder of what it is like for those that had to work in the trenches. He was treated well once his story was confirmed, but he sure paid the price to get there.

He was escorted to a rather large conference room. Inside, there were military commanders and agents scurrying back and forth around a large round table and lit-up map. He walked over to it and was greeted well by the President of the United States.

"On behalf of the United States government, I wish personally to thank you and present to you this medal of honor for the great service with which you have served this country."

Harrison slowly opened the box. It was a medal for valor. Harrison just stared at the medal. He didn't realize that the room had gone silent. Looking up, he caught everyone staring at him. Then one by one they all joined in for a round of applause.

After the applause subsided, they all patted him on the back in praise. He was still clutching the President's hand when he said very quietly, "Thank you, sir. It is the most beautiful thing ever given to me. But, sir, I am not the one who deserves this. The true hero was Bozinov."

"No, you do deserve it," the President replied. He gave Harrison one last firm handshake. "Bozinov will get a hero's memorial—that I can promise you. However, for now we are glad you are here." The President put his hand on Harrison's shoulder. "Now, let's begin our defense."

The President quickly became all business, walking over to the table and calling for quiet. He motioned for the general to speak.

"Mr. President, it is our opinion that our best defense is to hit them as hard as we can right at the border when they attempt to come across.

We can also make a show of force before they get there, not doing anything in secret. We will move our troops in the open, let them know we know they are coming. Hopefully when they realize we are aware of their plan, they will choose to avert this war by standing down, sir."

The President nodded in approval. "Very well. I hereby authorize the use of force. The general's plan is to be implemented as our main objective. General, begin the massive buildup of our forces in the north. I shall advise the Alliance members of our plans, particularly the Canadian government. Meanwhile, I want reinforcements sent to the south."

Picking up the red-colored phone, he said to the person at the other end of the line, "Recall all senators for an emergency session of Congress."

The President held his hands up to stop the pandemonium that was about to begin. "Gentlemen, ladies, you have your orders. Make us proud!"

A bunch of "yes, sirs" went out as the people quickly scurried away. The President, for his part, once again stared out the window at the people. "I am going to enact the draft. It's time to give these people something to believe in again. This place is still worth fighting for!"

Chapter 16

Hussad was having a back and foot rub by his many wives when the messenger came in. Last time it was bad news. *Might have to waste some scientists again*, he thought. He opened the sealed envelope and motioned the courier out.

This time it was good news. So it would seem that the Eastern and Western Alliances were about to embark on a little war. Grinning, he called for the guard to bring in his advisor.

Hussad began to get dressed quickly. He put on his best military outfit and, sitting at his desk, waited for his advisor.

The man came running in the office panting. Quickly he stopped and bent low to the earth in front of him before looking Hussad square in the face, a gesture that Hussad had come to demand of all that entered his presence.

Hussad motioned for him to sit down while he read the information he had. The advisor's eyebrows went up and his eyes became wide with wonder before they became slits like a snake.

Hussad eyed him coolly. He knew that look on the other man's face and he loved it. "So what do you think?" he asked, knowing full well the other man's answer. If there was one thing his advisor did, it was show his emotions.

"Perhaps there is an opportunity here," he began.

Hussad smiled at him and said, "Yes, you grasp my intentions well.

I believe it is time to bring to life the minds and hearts of the soldiers that I have spent much investment in."

"Of course, General. You are most wise!" he said and once again bowed.

The general appreciated the gesture, for it was both courteous and respectful.

The man looked up. "However, I would ask that the general please consider the possibility of an alliance with the US. This would, of course, not be a true alliance. We would make a show of friendship while secretly we operate covertly so as to seize their technology. We take it right out from under them while they are busy with their war."

The general pondered this for a moment before deciding. Then, with his mind made up, he spoke once more. "That is a good idea. However, I believe that it is in our best interests to let their own soldiers do the dirty work for us. That way we remain totally anonymous. Besides, it would take too long to develop such an alliance. No, we must act now. Enact the program."

Bowing his head, the advisor replied, "Yes, my lord."

Chapter 17

"Well, how did you like it?" Pam asked.

"Dinner was magnificent, but then it always is. You are such a good cook. You spoil me," Doug replied.

Pam's cheeks flushed with the compliment. "Thanks," she said. "I try hard to please my man."

"You don't have to try hard. You don't even have to try, you do anyway," he said.

He became self-conscious of all the dishes and mess that had been made for him that he asked her if he could help her clean up. Before she could reply, he got up and, walking over to the wall, turned on the lights. They had been sitting the whole time without the lights on, with only the single candle at the table with which to eat by.

She smiled despite the interruption to the romantic setting. He was only trying to be thoughtful and she loved him for it. However, tonight she had other thoughts, and they did not include dishes.

She got up and moved quickly to intercept him. She put her hand on his chest to stop him from moving. She could feel his heart beating under her hand. It beat strong and fast under her touch. She felt the shudder that went through his body at her soft fingers resting on him.

With her other hand, she reached up and turned off the light so that once more they were mostly in darkness. With her hand still on his chest, he brought his hand up to meet hers.

She took her hand off his chest and, holding it out in front of her, her eyes met his, waiting patiently, yet longingly for his touch.

His hand came up and very slowly began to touch his fingers to hers. Slowly at first, as the fleeting touch sent sensations coursing through them. Then his touch became more needy as he clasped his hand in hers, savoring the sensation.

Then slowly, with her hands still grasped in his, she began to pull him out of the kitchen and into the living room. The light from the candle shone dimly and its flickering made strange ghost-like shadows that danced upon the wall. Its light illuminated the pair like a halo from a heavenly source. Much like one would expect if one were to happen upon the image of an angel of God.

Pam pulled Doug down upon the floor and, kneeling down, they sat upon their knees facing one another. Once again, their hands reached out to touch one another, only this time they began to explore each other's bodies.

Doug's body began to ache as Pam's touch went through his skin and touched his very soul. She ran her fingers across his arms, his neck and his chest. The tender touch of such delicate fingers seared his flesh like fire.

He reached out to her, to grasp her cheeks and cup her face in his hands. Her skin was like rose petals, soft and delicate. Her hair spilled over her shoulders and upon his forearm. He could feel its silkiness as he reached up to run his fingers through it. His other hand stroked her cheek with compassion. His desire for her began to swell to the point of explosion. He needed to tell her how he felt. He began to speak, but Pam put a finger to his lips.

She hushed him silently with that gesture. Somewhere within her, the need to express how she felt beyond the words began to swell. She needed that from him too at that moment, and not words. He sensed that and did not resist. She began to move closer towards him, her hand still upon his lips as she moved ever closer, her lips towards his.

His arms went out and began to caress her upper body, hugging her close to him as she came ever closer to joining her moist lips against his. Their eyes never averted as they came closer to one another, tipping their heads so their lips could join.

She kissed him slowly, but not fully. Teasingly at first, she allowed her lips to brush against his and back again. She sensed his desire swell like that of a volcano as the pressure began to build. Her desire for him swelled too, watching his need to bring his lips into full contact with hers. Then with one desirous lunge he pulled her towards him, pressing his lips full upon her mouth.

Their lips parted, allowing their tongues to slip in between them. They moved their heads back and forth as their tongues stroked the inside of each other's mouths, sending spasms of pleasure coursing through their veins. They kissed for some time before finally moving to other parts of the body that would bring about sensual desire.

Doug's hand was upon Pam's shoulder as he slowly began to move it downward. Deliberately, his desire to touch her body and soul was more powerful than his fear, as his hands shook from the closeness. He watched her face as his hand moved upon one of her breasts, wanting, needing to see both the pleasure and approval that she would give him.

Her face showed the look of approval that he needed to see as the spasms of pleasure came from within her body from the touch. Her body also gave its approval as her nipples responded in like manner by becoming hard and reaching toward his touch. He could feel their bulge through her clothing as he brushed his hand back and forth upon them.

She moved her hands down upon her waist and, without taking her eyes from his, pulled her shirt off of herself. The cool air quickly hitting her skin made her shiver. But it didn't matter, his touch was warm and she longed for it. Grasping his hands once more, she pulled him downward on top of her.

Their bodies became engrossed with passion as their members became swelled and hot with desire for their joining. They made love that whole night long. They brought each other to ecstasy more than once that night. Each time their desires erupted in one explosion of passion, until finally their bodies, racked with sweat from exhaustion and utter fulfillment, lay entwined with one another, sleepily satisfied and feeling safe.

Chapter 18

The sky was filled with dark shadow clouds that were low in the sky and menacing. They were bulky and moved quickly in the wind. They, of course, were typical storm clouds, dropping torrents of water. The thunder cracked overhead and sent sonic booms hurtling through the airwaves. The scene was eerie, like the opening seconds of a horror film.

The men at the gatehouse to the army base were shivering. The one man hated this weather. It was dark, gloomy and depressing. Besides, he felt as if he would catch pneumonia. It always seemed that his shift came up on the most horrible of days for weather.

The door swung open and he curled himself up. The other guard came into the little gatehouse along with a wind and wet rain that chilled them to the bone. Slamming the door shut, he let out a big sigh.

"Whew, looks like we got a real good one going, eh?" the soldier said, taking off his rain cover.

"Yeah, great," the man replied moodily.

"Hey, what's with you?" the rather wet-looking soldier said. "Well, I guess I don't blame you. You do look rather peaked. Here, I got just the thing." The man sat down next to him and, reaching into his pocket, pulled out a flask and offered it to the man.

The other soldier snapped around. "Hey, we are on duty. I should report you for this!"

"Aw, come on, you want some or not?" The man holding the flask waved it teasingly around in front of the other soldier's face.

The man eyed him for a second, wrestling with his conscious, knowing full well he could get severely disciplined for this. However, he thought, *It's late, nobody usually comes in or out at this time of night.* If they did and he was drunk, he could pull himself together enough to salute and open the gate. He could give them the all-too-familiar wave of the hand. He reserved it for just such occasions. He did not want to go out and check IDs in the rain, and nobody wanted to roll down their window to let him. *So why not*, he thought. He really needed something to pick up his mood.

"Give me that," the man said, snatching the flask from the other man's grasp. He took it and gulped a large swallow, letting out a rather vulgar sound of approval when he was done.

"Yeah, there's plenty more where it came from, too," the other soldier said in approval of the man's final consensus. Reaching into his other pocket, he pulled out a whole bottle of whiskey. Opening it up, he clinked bottle to flask with the soldier and the two began to drink heavily, their spirits soaring higher and higher with the more spirits they poured into their very intoxicated bodies.

They did not mind now that the lightning flashed and the thunder cracked so loud it could almost shatter the windows of the little guardhouse. They took no notice. They did not notice anything going on around them except the words of the songs that they sung in cheer and the liquid that flowed down their throats. Neither did they notice the movement in the shadows just beyond the light of the guardhouse.

The men moved stealthily and assuredly through the brush. They took up their position just within thirty yards of the guardhouse, but out of view. They were well camouflaged and heavily armed. The militia never fooled around when it came to missions. Many of the members were from local parts, but some came from other states. Back in the day, they were just a bunch of local yahoos that hated the federal government. They would hole up in camps with all kinds of guns and bunkers and were regarded as radicals. They still were today, only now, they were organized across the country; they had helped in the crumbling of the United Nations, their first objective. Now they were again in one of the greatest maneuvers ever. No longer would they be radicals. They would be heroes of the free world.

The pact with the Eastern Alliance made some of the men uneasy, but when they had assurances of the Eastern Alliance's support for their idea of the federal government, they saw their duty clear. Perhaps they could restore world peace by removing the corrupt US government and replace it with a better one. One like their forefathers originally intended it to be.

One of the men wore a headset. Reaching down, he activated it and spoke to someone on the other end, telling them they were in position. One of the soldiers sitting next to him slipped off his backpack and opened it up, pulling out his rifle and a tripod. He set it down and hooked the night-vision scope up to it and sighted one of the men in the guardhouse. They had practiced this in one of their camps. They had set up a mock base just like the real one. Timing was going to be everything.

The truck came down the long road. The man driving the military vehicle was absolutely stoic in appearance. His thoughts did not drift. He could not afford them to. He knew what the payload of the nuclear device he carried in the back of the wagon was. He knew what would happen to him if he were caught with such a device. He needed total concentration, and that was what he had. He had his mind set on his mission: help his fellow comrades destroy that base.

He came driving up to the gate. Everything was set. They had practiced it a million times. The rain made it even better because he could get away with just giving a familiar wave to the man opening the gate. He did not want to get wet any more than need be. He slowed his truck, bringing it to a halt just in front of the gate.

The soldiers in the gatehouse stopped singing and tried to pull themselves together somewhat; the one man tried to sit up straight but was kind of wobbly. It was up to the other soldier to do his duty, letting the vehicle pass, and keep their butts out of hot water.

Getting up, the soldier with the flask tucked the flask in his pocket and did his best to try and be military-like in his walk. An all-too-familiar wave came from the vehicle. *Thank God*, the man thought. *I don't think I could have pulled this off.* Walking just outside to the gate control, he pushed the button, triggering the mechanism which opened the gate.

The truck pulled inside and, when it had cleared, the soldier hit the button again, closing the fence. The noise of the moving gate and the storm drowned out the small sound of a bullet piercing the glass of the gatehouse and lodging itself in the forehead of the other soldier. The man fell face forward onto the desk, no longer able to trigger any alarms.

As the soldier tried to make his way back to the gatehouse, wrapping the coat around him, the truck suddenly stopped. Its engine turned off. The soldier stopped and, looking back at the truck, heard someone yell out, "I seem to be having a problem. Can you give me a hand?"

The man stood still for a second, then looked back in the direction of the gatehouse, where he longed to be. He could see the other soldier slumped over the desk. *Drunk, no doubt,* he assumed. So it was going to be up to him. With his head still spinning, he walked over to the truck where he thought he would meet up with the driver. Instead, he found the driver pointing a handgun at him. Quickly he became sober, but it was too late. With his eyes wide as he looked incredulously at the other man, he was felled with a silenced shot to the chest.

The man driving the truck quickly dragged the man over to the side and hit the button opening the gate, where another truck was waiting. Picking up the dead man, he carried him inside the gatehouse where he was joined by his companions from the other vehicle.

"You know what to do," he told them. Quickly snapping to the task at hand, they began to undress the dead soldiers, so they could switch clothes and take their place.

The driver of the truck opened the back of the truck to reveal a rather large metallic-looking device. Opening the cover, he flipped a switch activating the device. A display came up and he keyed in several codes. He replaced the cover and closed the back of his truck.

He moved quickly, getting into the truck and speeding off down the road. He left the other men at the gatehouse. They were to wait for him to drop off the bomb, set the detonator and come back.

However, he had no intention of such foolishness. Little did they realize that the very device he carried was nuclear. It did not matter if they were ten miles away when it went off. They were dead anyway. Everything within a twenty-mile radius was going to die. The farther from the blast, the longer it would take to die. So it was better this way.

When they first approached the militia group, they had made lots of promises. They had poured a lot of time and money into the group, all in an effort to gain their friendship. There were times though when they thought it might not be worth dealing with them, but now at the end, it was. They could never have pulled it off without the militia's help. They had bought into all of the Eastern Alliance's lies.

Subsequently, they did not tell them that the bomb was nuclear and they were all going to die when the blast went. He, too, would die, but it was a sacrifice for what he believed in. It was, of course, for the greater good.

The man sighed. "Oh well, going to die sometime anyway. At least it won't drag me out slow," he said rather resolutely.

He was getting closer to his final destination. There in front of him, he could see the long tunnel that would begin to go underground. The lights that were at the checkpoint gates inside the base began to come into view. He was going to blow through the gates in an effort to ram the bomb literally down the base's throat. That way he could be assured that the protection that the base had against nuclear attack would not withstand the blast.

He pulled the remote control from within his pocket and pushed a small button on it. This activated the sixty-second timer on the bomb.

Somewhere in the back of the truck, a small lighted panel on a nuclear device suddenly came alive. It showed a timer counting down from sixty, fifty-nine, fifty-eight....

The gate was close now. The army personnel was holding up his hand, signaling the truck to stop. Hitting the gas to the floor, he shifted the truck into the passing gear and just barely missed hitting the man in front of the gate who barely had time to get out of the way. The truck bulldozed the gate in front of him, blasting it apart. The army guard pulled out his gun and fired at the truck as it sped off in the direction of its quest.

Moving with haste, his hat flying off of his head, he went into the guardhouse and quickly sounded an alarm about the speeding truck.

The driver was coming into the tunnel now. A siren went off and he could see a several other gates closing. He rammed into one, shattering it. There were people accumulating ahead in front of him. All that he could hear was the sound of voices yelling, gunfire and the klaxon droning out the roar of his engine as he flew down the tunnel towards eternity.

The soldiers in front of him let fly a barrage of bullets that ripped through the truck, tearing the metal away from it as it came ever closer. A large metal door was trying to close behind the line of soldiers. Its movement was slow going, too slow for the crisis at hand. They hoped it would close in time, willing it somehow in their minds so as to escape the fate that would await those underground.

With his body bleeding and his hair blowing, the needle buried on the speedometer, the driver met his eternity.

The vehicle came crashing to a final halt as it lodged itself between the door and the door jamb, sending shrapnel into the closest of people around. The door was crushing the truck like a car masher at a junkyard. If only there were a few more seconds, it would sever the truck in two, as it was bent on its mission of closing. The device for its part was unscathed. Ten, nine, eight….

The two men at the guardhouse were beginning to get edgy. "Where is he?" the one asked the other.

"How should I know?" the other replied.

"I don't like this, I'm calling for backup." Pulling a transceiver out of his pocket, he tried to contact the other parties outside the base.

"That's right, I think it's a bust. I want you to extract us….Don't argue with me. Look, we are in trouble here. We need help!"

Those were the last words uttered, and the last words ever heard by anyone of the militia group. The blast was so great they barely heard the explosion before they were vaporized.

The blast ripped through everything in its wake, sending a mushroom cloud ten miles into the sky, spewing radioactive ash across the face of the ground where it had already ripped the earth and anything upon it to shreds. The light from the blast was so bright that .

anyone twenty miles away would be instantly blinded, their very eyes burning from their sockets should they see it for only a moment.

However, there was nobody to see. This had been a very strategically placed base, right in the middle of the desert. Nobody would know, at least not until it was too late. There were two other very similar earth-shattering quakes not too long in succession after that, thus, marking a successful mission by the Alliance.

The attacks were necessary to remove the US military's ability to respond quickly. The US would be too busy trying to figure out what happened. All the while, the true objective was the base where the child experiment was going on. The three target bases were closest and moving troops between them was easily done. Now, of course, it made the main target, for all practical purposes, all alone.

Somewhere in a small cubicle, a lone recorder recorded seismic activity on paper. The news the next day from the US Center of Geological Survey would report a quake in California registering 4.6 on the Richter scale.

Nobody suspected that a commercial airline carrier could be a transport plane for troops as one by one lone parachutes carrying men floated noiselessly out from the clouds. There were at least five hundred troops. It would be more than enough to take the main base, especially since it would be by surprise.

The militia would be of help as well, having already planted the necessary bombs in the correct strategic places around the base. All they had to do was detonate them remotely.

The troops moved quickly towards their objective: the base, the child, and victory.

Chapter 19

General John Bass was taking a nap when the communication link came to life. He brought the computer online and the screen was flooded with a wealth of encrypted information. Quickly running the message through the decoder, he got the information pertaining to the current situation.

The base was supposed to be on full military alert. It was, and yet it was more important to have all troops transported to the front than to defend the base. There was only so much that he would have to worry about in the middle of the desert.

The communication that was sent to the upper command was much more informative than those of the lower ranks. Rank definitely had its privileges, so he got to read all about Harrison. The news, of course, was very encouraging. It would seem that the Eastern Alliance was about to get handed a major defeat. However, he was ordered to maintain full military alertness.

He let out a sigh of relief. "Full military alertness, eh?" he said as he yawned.

This was going to be a short one. It was a shame that it had to happen at all. He began to get dressed and then sent orders to his staff to begin recalling people from the base houses to inside the mountain.

It did not take long before an alarm went out and people began moving frantically to and fro about the base. Special teams were set up to help deal with moving large quantities of people from the base residences to the main part of the base, which was deep within the mountain.

Chapter 20

Pam had collected a bunch of baby things into the diaper bag which was flopping around on her shoulder. She was holding the baby and a ton of other things at once. There was no time to pack so she was quickly trying to get as much stuff as possible. The baby was in a diaper only. Shoving things into the bag, she began to talk aloud to herself, "Let's see…diapers, ointment, some wipes, towels, blankets."

Some military personnel came through the door. They were all stiff and serious looking. This, of course, sent the baby into a crying fit from fear.

Pam was angry. "Don't you people know how to knock! You scared him!"

"Sorry, ma'am. We have orders to take you and the child to the secure area inside the mountain."

"That is not the point. There are no enemy personnel in my living room. Don't tell me you could not have knocked."

"Umm, sorry, ma'am," was all the soldier could muster in response to her rather brash attitude.

Pam let out an exasperated sigh. *Bunch of military mongrels. They have camouflage for brains*, she thought.

The soldiers took out the things that she had piled by the door. Grabbing the baby, she was escorted out the door by armed escorts. The baby was crying from all the noise. He was afraid.

"Shhh," she said, cradling him in her arms and rocking him as they drove off in an army jeep. "It's ok. Mommy is here. It's okay."

They had driven into the mountain and were escorted down an elevator and down onto the floor where the lab existed. They had a room all prepared with a bed and a crib. Under any other circumstance, especially one such as this—where one child was to be the savior of the human race—such an important individual would have already been kept under the strictest of security in the mountain. However, Pam had made such a fuss to anyone and everyone, they had decided to let her have her way.

Pam put the baby down and nodded to the troops as they closed the door behind her. She began to try to make the room as comfortable as possible. It was good for her to be going about such business. She, too, was afraid.

Where is Doug? she wondered. She desperately wanted to feel his strong arms around her, and let her know it was all right. But he wasn't and she needed to be strong now, so she continued to get things ready, and before she knew it, she had everything unpacked. Finding herself with nothing to do, she watched Adam looking at the new environment he found himself in and began playing.

Pam wished she were that innocent. She wished she did not know about any of this. She hated war and violence, which was somewhat of a contradiction in her life. Here she was, a mind firmly set against the use of military and its pig-headed ideals, while all along she was working for the government in a military base.

I must be crazy, she thought. She attempted a smile in spite of herself. At least they treated her good. It was a lot better than a lot of people on the outside got. She looked at the green metal door and the tan cinder block walls with no windows, all very prison/military decorum. *All the comforts of home, well, sort of,* she thought and sighed.

Chapter 21

Polov was looking out the window. He knew about the report of the Western Alliance's quick troop movement response. It could mean only one thing. The Hunter had failed. That was why they had lost contact with him. He must have been killed and Bozinov had escaped. *Strange*, he thought. His operatives within the borders of the West would no doubt have spotted him. Perhaps it was that Bozinov was dead along with the Hunter, but had managed to leak the information to someone else. It was a mystery. The news greatly disturbed him. He was so sure that he could contain Bozinov, who was an imbecile.

"Instead he made a fool out of me," he muttered. *I underestimated him and was too overconfident. I shall not do that again. Although, it seems the operation regarding our paratroopers has been successful. It could be that only part of the message was leaked or....*

His eyes closed slightly at the thought that began to burn in his mind. His mouth twitched as his teeth ground together, and his hands became fists. "Or perhaps there is another informant," he said aloud.

His mind began to race. *There are infinite possibilities*, he thought. Quickly, the part of his brain that was easily triggered into mania took over. He began to obsess on the idea that there had to be someone else.

Perhaps I can catch him. Bozinov must surely be dead. If I can expose Bozinov and the other one in our ranks, I can salvage all of this and be a real hero. But who can it be? Bozinov was the only one who made any objections at the meeting.

With a flash of anger, he said slowly and menacingly, "This man is good! Bozinov was surely a fool, but not, not this man."

He began to work himself into frenzy, pacing back and forth, talking to himself, sometimes almost arguing with himself. Faster and faster he talked as he paced around the room. He was in an altered state of reality where paranoia, mania and fear drove his actions and thoughts.

"He is a devil!" he yelled aloud, then whirling around upon someone behind him that wasn't there, he said, "But I will catch you!" He was yelling now, pointing at the air as if he saw an apparition before him and was pointing and talking to it. There was, of course, nobody there, but the whole scene was enough to send chills through any sane man watching.

Then, suddenly and abruptly, he stopped. He let his hand fall and he straightened his tunic. "I will catch you. I will be watching for ones like you. You would be on the surface loyal to our cause, but sooner or later you will come out. I will trust nobody and suspect everybody. Sooner or later you will attempt to stop what we are doing, and then, then you will be mine."

He turned on his heel and walked back to his desk and sat down. There was still much to do. He had to make adjustments in the current military lines so as to meet the Western's defense positions. He needed to go all out on the front for two very good reasons. One, he wanted to break their lines, and two, he could draw all attention away from the ultimate objective.

One of the general's subordinates came into his office at that moment. The man stood at attention in front of his desk waiting for his superior officer to address him. It was, of course, military protocol, even though he had known the man for years and was one military stripe under him.

Polov never looked up from his writing. He merely addressed the man. "General, these are the new military positions you are to take." He handed him a sheet of paper.

The other officer was somewhat dumbfounded as he took the paper, he was himself a brilliant strategist—something Polov knew. The fact that Polov had not consulted him was somewhat perplexing, especially since the troops were under his direct command. He took the paper and began to read. His jaw dropped open at the new deployment. There were no defensive positions. He knew full well the current status of the Western readiness and this stance wasn't even a stance—it was suicide.

"Sir..." he stammered. "Sir, I don't understand, these positions, they are, uh....Sir, begging the general's pardon, sir. Is the general informed on the current military positions of the West?"

"Yes, I am soldier. You have your orders, carry on," Polov said without looking up at the man.

The other officer didn't understand. Up until that point, Polov had never behaved in such a way. It was his duty to question his superior officer's orders, as he was ordering many men to their deaths. Although it bordered on insubordination, he pressed on. "General, I must protest this military strategy."

Polov actually looked up at the man then and eyed him. His demeanor was staunch, his face devoid of all emotion. "General," he said slowly, "I am aware of the current potential military losses. I am aware that the current defensive positions of the enemy will cause heavy losses onto our troops, but we can break those lines. They have not been fully formed yet."

"Yes, but at what cost? We look at a battle won but...General, hundreds of thousands will die. This is not a war, it is a bloodbath!"

Polov was not amused. He had not gotten to where he was by worrying about loss of life, even that of his own troops. "You don't come in here and tell me about loss of life, you come in here and take those orders and follow them, is that clear?" Polov went back to his writing without waiting for an answer from the man. He considered the matter closed. It was also a dismissal from his office.

The other man just stood there and stared at Polov. *He is mad*, he thought. He shook his head. This was madness. He was a soldier not a butcher. He decided that there was nothing he could do but inform Polov that he would go over him if he continued in this line of action. He had known him for years, but he'd never known him to act in such a way. Why would he go all out to win a battle, when the main objective was the child?

Polov knew, of course. It was his need for world domination, his secret passion for torture and to watch it, his need to control, to enslave, to be a god himself. Too many he was a god. He must succeed, this would be the pinnacle of his career. His vision of world unification was in his own delusional mind bigger than any before him. Hitler had the right idea of a world order, but his vision on how to attain had been much too narrow. It was not enough to defeat the army and take the capital. No, you had to break the enemy's back along with it. Beaten but not defeated was the motto. His way was beaten and defeated. This way he could then help rebuild alongside the enemy and get them to appreciate him for helping them. Then they would be loyal. He had to crush the other army regardless of how many soldiers it took. That way he would secure a place in history as one of the greatest leaders to do what no man had been able to do. He had to achieve the technology of the child so he could be a hero to the common man.

"General Polov, I came in here to inform you it would seem that the western forces have taken up key defense positions just south of our troops. Our military commanders have received a direct communiqué from the opposing side informing us that they are aware of our presence and order us to stand down. General, we must withdraw our forces."

"What!" Polov's pen dropped out of his hand onto the desk as he stood up quickly in anger. "Withdraw? Now, in our finest hour? I think you underestimate the ability of our troops and our ultimate goal."

"But, sir, this is suicide! They are aware of us! If you do not withdraw, I will go to the First Secretary himself and have you arrested for this…this crime you are about to commit!"

Polov's eyes went wide in a moment of surprise then quickly a dark shadow covered his face. He knew now. It had been him all along.

"So you are the one. It wasn't Bozinov at all," Polov said quietly and slowly.

The other man shook his head. He had no idea what Polov was talking about, for it was all in Polov's mind.

"Sir, what one? I don't understand. What about Bozinov, sir? You and I have worked together for many years."

"As if you didn't know," Polov said, looking at him with a smirk on his face. Polov knew to look for a man that would try to stop what he would be doing, but he had not expected him to be so easy to pick. Of course, he could prove nothing. "You are a traitor, General. Those front lines are immaterial and the technology is everything. It was you that leaked the information to the West. You are the one that made sure that army was there waiting for us so that you could come marching in here. Then you would preach to me about loss of life and get me to acquiesce and assure a victory for yourself and your Western Alliance friends. Well, I think not!"

The other man stood in total disbelief, shaking his head. He couldn't think of anything to say other than, "You are mad."

The two men just stood there staring at one another for a long moment—one with hatred and contempt in his eyes, the other in total revulsion. Then, quickly, the lower general turned on his heels to walk out as he said, "I am going to put a stop to this!"

Polov turned around and pulled his handgun out of his coat and cocked it.

The sound stopped the other man dead in his tracks.

"Neither you nor anyone else will stop me," Polov said as he aimed directly at the back of the other man.

The other man whirled around. "You will never get away with it."

Polov grinned. "On the contrary..." he said and, turning the gun toward himself, pulled the trigger. The bullet was aimed well enough to just graze him; however, it did not keep him from falling down in pain. Partially propping himself up, he took the gun he had and threw it at his nemesis.

The man was so dumbfounded at everything that had happened that he just caught the gun as the door swung open to reveal the guards who came because of the shot.

Polov yelled out, "Help me! He's armed. Shoot him! He is a traitor. Help!"

The other man was in shock, but when he came out of it, he tried to yell as well but it was too late. The guard was acting on instinct alone and let fly a barrage of bullets into the man.

The soldier ran to General Polov, helping him to his feet.

"General, are you alright?" he asked.

"Yes, he just grazed me. He was a traitor, he was the one who informed the Western Alliance of our troop movement. When I caught him, he tried to kill me."

The other man gently lifted Polov to his seat. The soldier looked up to Polov. He was one of the god worshipers, for to him Polov could do no wrong.

"I am so glad you acted as quickly as you did. Thank you, you are a good soldier!" He patted the man on the back with his good arm.

The soldier just beamed, for he was a hero and would no doubt be rewarded by Polov. Perhaps he would get a medal or even a promotion. Collecting himself quickly, the guard yelled to one of his fellow officers to get the doctor.

Polov thanked him again and sat down at his desk to bring his communication device online. He instructed the office at the other end to send forth the commandos to assault the base in the southern US and begin the ground war in the north, per the following instructions.

Chapter 22

The alarm klaxon had been sounding. People were moving very quickly as red flashes of light from the alarm signals made the whole scene seem that much more perilous.

General Bass went over to the person behind the desk. "What is our status?" he asked.

"Sir, enemy forces are approaching the base."

"Bring all units online, prepare to repel assault. Get me the President on the line, I need to let them know we are under attack.

"Yes, sir," the army major said in reply. The major pushed a few buttons and nodded to the red-colored phone for the conference call with the President. The major put a headset on and began to communicate troop movements and strategy plans to the infantry.

"Mr. President, this is General Bass. Sir, we are under heavy attack."

Meanwhile, on the northern border of Canada, a huge battle had begun; the onslaught was a bloodbath as troops recklessly charged at the West's dug-in forces. It was a suicide attempt in an effort to eventually overrun the West's lines. After constant bombardment and heavy loss of life, the Eastern forces managed to break through the loosely created defense line and were advancing.

"Yes, sir, Mr. President," General Bass concluded and hung up the phone. Although they were aware of the war plan of the Eastern Alliance, the new attack on their base had caught them off guard, .

because no one would expect a hit on a military base well within national borders. The timing could not have been worse as many of his troops had been sent to the north to shore the defense the West was making. He did not have even a quarter of his command.

However, it was better to have some military alertness than none. Had they not known any of the plans, if Harrison had not been able to warn them, it would have been a much different battle. A chill went up Bass's spine and made him shudder at the thought.

Although the collapsed line in the north was forced to retreat, the military alertness and the determination of the US troops began to plug the holes in the line of the defenders. Slowly but surely, they began to overwhelm the assailants and push them outward, regaining lost ground. The President and all involved at the Oval Office smiled at the satellite readouts of the battle. It was the first and biggest smile he had given all day long. He knew then that it was going to be a total rout of the enemy. They would either be forced to surrender eventually or they would be killed in battle; it made no difference now. However, he quickly recomposed himself as he remembered the other battle ensuing. He had ordered reinforcements to the secret experimental base but it would take time. Was it possible that the war was a diversion? Had he made a mistake? Only time would tell.

A brigade from the 33rd airborne division was advancing from the rear of the enemy, cutting off their escape. They had been dispatched immediately as soon as Bass called into the President to inform him of the assault. NORAD was aware of the decisive destruction of the other bases and had ordered the military to secure the radioactive area. They had dispatched part of that division to Bass's Base, as they liked to call it. The general allowed himself a small sigh of relief, knowing that help was on the way. He put his top military strategist in charge of cleaning up and went back to his office.

A cheer went up from within the Oval Office that could be heard outside. The joint chiefs and many of the other military officials and elected officers from the Western Alliance were all talking and laughing all at once. Their chatter was all brought about by a simple message from the front lines.

"Mr. President, our troops are beginning to advance on the enemy, sir. We are pushing them back."

This was, of course, cause for good cheer. Tensions had been high and each man and woman knew what would have happened to the alliance had they been caught off guard. The size of the army was enormous. Although, size of an army does not matter as much with military technology. But being unprepared makes a big difference. They all owed a debt of gratitude to one man—Harrison. Someone actually suggested some champagne.

The President was not celebrating. He was a man of thought. He stared out his window and thought hard. He thought so hard it hurt. He kept on asking himself the same question—why?

Someone approached him to talk to him, but stopped short when they could sense the President's mood. The person who was the joint chief of staff, seeing the whole thing, picked up a glass of champagne. Walking over to the President, he offered it to him. "You look like a man who really needs a drink, but not for the reason we do."

The President took the glass from the man but did not drink it. He just held it very tightly in his grasp. "I don't think we should be celebrating just yet."

"Why? Sir, we are going to win this one."

Drawing in a deep breath through his nose and letting it out slowly with his head tilted up so that he could feel the muscles in his upper back, he said, "I know. But something just isn't right." Suddenly snapping around, the President asked, "Where is Harrison?"

Harrison walked up to him and sat down. The President looked at him and said, "Harrison, this country owes you a great debt. However, I still have some concerns and I want your thoughts on them."

Harrison was somewhat surprised over the President's cautiousness. He was all into the celebration, thinking it was over.

"I feel that something is wrong. Why this attack? Why the blatant foolishness of it all? Is there anything else you know about Bozinov?" the President asked.

Harrison tried to recall anything and shook his head; it was all becoming a blur now, the whole chase, Bozinov's death on the hillside.

"Who did he work for?" the President asked.

"Polov," Harrison replied.

The President put his hand up to his head and rubbed his temples. Then, suddenly, he sat upright. "They aren't here for war, they are here…" he never finished his sentence. Hitting the intercom, he brought up the general at NORAD and told him that the main assault to gain control of the experiment was merely a diversion. He knew now that the secondary assault on the base with the child was the main objective. It all became clear. It explained the other bases being destroyed. They had no idea who had destroyed those bases. Now it was clear that the Eastern Alliance was to blame for it. It allowed them to get troops in from the south. Although that base could normally hold its own in a battle, it was short on troops. He just hoped that they could get there in time.

Kirk and his soldiers were unpacking all their gear in one of the ammunition rooms. They had been one of the key teams in stopping the Alliance's assault on their base. He was so proud of them. He knew that help was a couple of hours away at least and they had held their ground against a terrible onslaught. His team performed well, without a single casualty.

They were all laughing and joking and slapping each other on the back. All this went on until one man sat down holding his head. The others did not notice him at first and then another went down as well. The laughing stopped then.

Kirk was going to order the man standing next to him to get a medical team when the man standing there also went down. All of his soldiers began to double over in pain, complaining of headaches of some sort. All of them were grasping their heads, all but Kirk.

He could not understand what was going on. It then occurred to him—some form of bio-warfare. Quickly, he got out their masks and put them on so that they breathed nothing but oxygen. He informed them to stay put and ran to get help.

As abruptly as the headache had come, it stopped. Only now they had a new sense of well-being, a new destiny. They understood now. Awakened from their deep sub-conscious was that which was programmed years ago by the Afim.

Pulling off the masks, they knew what they had to do. Quickly they gathered their armaments and moved down the hall toward the communications room. They knew that Kirk would be back soon so they left one of theirs to deal with him.

They marched double time to the communication center. There was only one man in the room and he greeted them cordially as they filtered in.

"What's up, guys?" he asked, smiling.

"I wanted to show my friends here a little about the way these devices work. So I was wondering if you wouldn't mind giving them a little bit of a tour?"

The other man was a little surprised, as they were still technically at war and the timing of it was bad. *Still*, he thought, *what the heck, we won the war*, and delighted over the idea, as no one had ever asked him to do a demo of the equipment before.

"Of course," he replied enthusiastically. He began to talk a bit about how it all worked. As soon as he turned around to talk about some piece of equipment, one of the men grabbed his head with one hand and gave it a fatal twist with the other.

Stuffing him in the back room, they brought the equipment online and sent a message directly to the African Republic, acknowledging their program activation and requested instructions, after which they destroyed the equipment. No messages were getting in or out.

Locking the door as they left and with branded tattoos that they had put onto their skin, the infiltrators—as they would come to be known—went to find General Bass.

Chapter 23

The little party had been going on some time at the White House, as they were all celebrating not only one victory in the north, but two because the base in the south had held its own against the Alliance. They were all still patting each other on their backs when an aide came busting in. "Mr. President, Mr. President!"

The whole room had stopped what conversation they were engaged in when the frantic man came bustling through the room.

"What is it?" the President asked.

"Sir, satellite communication monitoring has picked up a direct communication between someone within the biological research military base and the African Republic's government. They did not bother disguising their message with encryption or anything, just straight airwaves."

The man handed the President the message. The President was about to read it when he asked, "No encryption, nothing? Are you sure this is authentic?"

"Yes, sir, confirmed across two listeners."

The President began to read the message aloud:

"Our Queen Goddess Kahli, her servants do await our instructions."

The reply:

"In accordance with the ways of the Afim, you are to bring to ruin those that would oppose our calling. Namely the Christian life-givers. They are our enemy. They oppose us. Their experiments, their scientists, their research, must be destroyed. Death to them that oppose us, death to all."

The room was completely silent. Every man and woman stood silently still, for all their hopes had rested on the child that had been miraculously reproduced in that research facility. They had so gallantly protected it against the Eastern invaders, but now....

"Has a dispatch been sent to General Bass at the base?" the President asked.

"Sir, we can't raise the base through any communication. We sent someone to go in there directly, but it will be at least two hours before they get there. All troop vehicles are currently away from the area. We began pulling them back from the base when we heard the news that the base had withstood the attack."

The President suddenly felt a real sense of foreboding. Pulling the troops back had been a blundering military mistake. Walking silently across the room, all eyes upon him, he knew they were wishing somehow, someway, their leader, whom they put their faith in, would save them.

Walking over to the window, the President once again stared out of the window at the many street dwellers. He had felt earlier that he had failed them. They had put their trust in him and he had failed, just like he had failed those that were in the room with him. They looked to him for answers, they had elected him to lead, but it was all vanity. He thought, *A child, a savior, was born to us, and they killed him thousands of years ago. Now history may repeat itself. Only this time, this second chance may very well be the last. There is just not enough forethought available to man to foresee his own folly. There is no more future and no more hope.*

"God help us," was all he could say.

Chapter 24

Kirk came back with the doctor, but found only one soldier. As he entered the room, he started to reassure his men that it would be okay when he stopped short.

"Where is everyone, what happened?" he asked the one lone soldier standing there.

The soldier, fumbling over his words, replied, "Oh, uh, it is okay. They went to join in the cleanup from the fighting," and motioned for Kirk to go in the direction he pointed.

Kirk knew something was wrong. His men never disobeyed a direct order and he had told them to stay where they were. Kirk knew the statement was bogus and asked, "What cleanup?"

Being keenly aware of the body movements of the soldier, Kirk began to walk in that direction. He then made one quick motion with his arm that deflected the other man's attempt to stab him with a knife. He then brought his fist across the other man's jaw, sending him flying backward.

But the soldier wasn't a rookie. As he rolled, he pulled out a gun from his jacket. Pointing it at Kirk, his finger tightening on the trigger, he felt a sharp pain in his arm. He had forgotten about the doctor. The soldier stared at the empty syringe sticking out of his arm that had been injected into him. His eyes rolled back in his head and he slumped to the ground in a slumber.

"Good work," Kirk said, letting out his breath. He rolled the man over and let out a gasp. The doctor did not understand what he was seeing. The man had cut a mark into his chest, an upside-down V.

"Oh my God!" Kirk blurted.

"What?!" the doctor demanded.

Kirk did not explain other than mutter a single word as he fled from the room, "Afim."

The doctor's eyebrows went up. He had never heard of such a thing. Opening his bag, he went to work on treating for infection on the self-inflicted tattoo.

Kirk bolted from the room. He needed to talk to the general. The base had to be put on full alert. The men were incredibly dangerous. He did not understand. *How did it happen?* his mind screamed over and over. He had served with them for years. They just came out of battle together. Then it came to him. *The headaches*, he thought. *It has to be. Maybe somehow they are being controlled.*

The thought itself was almost rejected from his mind as being preposterous, for they had concluded long ago that such control of another person was impossible. Yet, it was the only conclusion he could reach. "These men are a real threat," he said aloud as he ran.

He knew now what was happening. He didn't know how, but somehow all of the men were tied to the Afim, and all of them were trained in special forces.

General John Bass was at his desk when the infiltrators came in. The general at first assumed they were there to assist in any way he wished and were reporting for some assignment.

The general stood up in his command stance. "What have you to report, men?"

"We no longer report to you or anyone else here," one soldier responded, then added, "sir," almost spitting it. The man pointed a gun at the general.

The general couldn't believe it. His face turned all red. After all, he was a general and they were his subordinates.

"What is the meaning behind all this?!" he demanded.

He quickly got the meaning when one of the soldiers jammed the barrel of a machine gun in his gut.

"We are your worst nightmare, do you get the meaning now?" the one soldier said. This brought about several chuckles and rather wicked-looking grins from the rest of the group.

"Guard, help me!" the general yelled, but the others were upon him to shut him up.

"There is no use yelling. There are no guards in this area, we took care of them," the soldier said, grinning again.

The soldiers' attitudes were smug and gruff. He acted, they all acted, as if they were part of a street gang and not soldiers. Gone was the discipline, gone the loyalty and the pride. Only hatred and a cold-blooded attitude that projected a murderous air about them remained.

"What do you want?" said the general.

Chapter 25

Doug knocked on the door and peeked in on Pam as she was playing with the child. She was singing to him a silly tune that made him smile and laugh. She then began to tickle him that put him into such a fit of laughter that both Doug and Pam could not help but forget for a moment the crisis that was going on outside.

"I am so glad you are here safe," he said as he took Pam in his arms.

"I know I am safe as long as you are here," she said, hugging him close.

Although she said she felt safe, she felt only safe there in his arms. The whole ordeal scared her to death. Not only for her life, but for everyone involved. She cared about them so much that she could not bear the thought of anything happening to them. Her eyes began to swell as the pent-up emotion finally released itself in tears.

Doug could tell that she was crying on his shoulder. He did his best to comfort her, holding her close and reassuring her. He stroked her silky hair and kissed her head, as he told her that he was there.

She responded to his assurances by wrapping herself around him even tighter. She cried and held him like that for a half an hour or more. Then when the tears were gone, she drew back and looked in his eyes.

He reached up one hand and wiped away the final teardrop that had spilled down her cheek.

"I love you," she said.

"I love you too," he replied and embraced her again.

CHAPTER 26

Kirk came rushing down the corridor. The hallways were empty. *Where is everybody?* he thought. *This is getting creepy.*

He stopped in front of one of the offices and called out, "Hello, hello, anybody here?"

There was no answer. He kept going deeper into the office when suddenly the door opened from the back room. The noise made Kirk jump in fear. Grabbing for his gun, he pointed in the direction of a surprised visitor. It was a secretary.

The secretary was just as afraid as Kirk was, if not more so, because she let out a blood-curdling scream. Despite his training, Kirk, at the sound of her scream, screamed too, and barely kept from pulling the trigger and accidentally shooting her. When this was done, both were breathing hard and in shock.

"Sorry. I didn't mean to scare you," Kirk gasped.

The woman, breathing hard as well, said, "That's ok...going to put the gun down?"

"Oh...." Kirk let the gun drop to his side. Composing himself, he asked, "Where is everybody? Where is Dr. Anderson? Where is General Bass?"

"Whoa, whoa, whoa, slow down. I don't know where everyone is. I have been here in the file room all day. Dr. Anderson went to Washington to give some presentation with one of the committees there. I haven't seen Bass, did you try his office?"

"Ok, thanks," was all he said as he ran out of the room leaving the secretary behind.

"You're welcome, have a nice day," she said sarcastically after him.

Kirk started to round the corner of the hallway where the general's office was, but quickly he jumped back when he recognized all of the usual guards were gone and replaced with his men, or used-to-be men.

Ok, Kirk, what do I do? he thought.

Kirk was good at his job. He knew that the men would die for their cause. He knew they were good at what they did, for he had trained them. They were some of the best. Now he regretted their training, but there was no time for regrets. He had to focus on what he was doing, and since they would be watching for him, he had to be more conniving then ever.

Taking only a moment to think, he looked up and saw the access panel to the crawl space between the drop ceiling and the roof truss. He climbed the ladder, pushed open the door and crawled up.

It did not take him long to get his bearings. He moved swiftly but quietly along the truss. Then, suddenly, as he was moving along, he stopped short when he could hear the conversation between the infiltrators and the general.

Slowly now, he crept up to where one of the florescent light fixtures was mounted onto the ceiling. Looking closely, he could see between the cracks of the fixture and the ceiling into the room.

"What do you want?" the general asked the one soldier.

The soldier who had done all the talking for the others nodded to them and they all began to unbutton their shirts. As each one showed his chest, Kirk could see where each man had tattooed himself with an upside-down V.

"The Afim!" the general said aghast.

"That's right, the Afim," replied the soldier. "I have been waiting for this moment to serve my leader and eliminate your kind for a long time. I have used your training, your weapons, for just this moment."

"You will never get away with it. If you think you four can defeat all the soldiers in this base...."

The other man started to laugh. "We have already taken this building. There is no one here left to help. Most of your troops are outside watching for the Eastern Alliance." The man talking got right in the face of the general, his piercing eyes a fire of hatred as he said, "General!" Stepping back from the general's face, he grinned smugly.

"What do you want?!" the general asked again.

"Your help," the man said matter-of-factly.

"Humph, yea right, you will get no help from me," the general said matter-of-factly.

"Oh, you are going to help alright." The man folded his arms across his chest and nodded his head.

The general snorted. He was grinning now. "I would rather die."

"That may come later," replied the soldier. He nodded to one of the other Afims. "Come here, General, I want to whisper something in your ear." The other Afim soldier pulled him to the first.

Kirk witnessed the whole thing—the hypnotic suggestion that the soldier said to him, the hypodermic needle that was pushed into the general's arm, and how General Bass told them everything, including where the child was. Horrified, he quickly began to back up to go warn someone. He was going to need some help.

As he was moving, he must have knelt on a soft spot because the beam let out a loud creak. He stopped suddenly, moving his weight all on his other leg, as it began to give him a cramp.

Everyone in the room went silent, looking up at the ceiling. Their eyes shifted between each other as they began to spread out from one another in the room. Each man was tightly clutching his firearm.

Kirk tried very hard to bring his other leg down quietly so he could continue to move but it was no use. The beam let out a noise that was unmistakable.

The men immediately began firing their guns at the ceiling, turning the air into a fog of shredded paper from the drop tiles. Kirk wasted no time moving from side to side as he avoided the bullets. He brought his own gun around and crashed though the ceiling while firing. He managed to get two of them while the other two ran out of the door.

"General, General, snap out of it!" he said, shaking the man.

Chapter 27

Doug got up to leave.

"You aren't going yet, are you? I'm afraid so. I want you to stay," she implored.

"I have to meet Dr. Tate in the lab. We are supposed to move forward with Operation Eve, seeing that Adam seems to be fine."

"Why are you doing this now? Aren't you afraid of moving ahead? What if we have to evacuate?"

Doug put up his hands to calm her down. "At last report, the troops had more than contained the Eastern Alliance. I have to get back to work." The look on her face said he better be gentle. "Besides, they won't evacuate us from here. We are more safe here under the mountain. I won't be gone long and you can come get me anytime you wish. I promise nothing bad is going to happen."

"You promise?" she asked.

"I promise," he said and kissed her forehead.

"Please come back soon," she said with a big sigh.

"I will return as soon as I finish." He grinned. "Bye, bye," he said, while waving to the baby.

Pam took the baby's arm and waved back.

Doug walked down the different hallways and into the lab.

Dr. Tate was waiting for him "On time as always I see," she said rather smugly.

"Warm and friendly as always, Joan," he replied, grinning back at her.

"Well, I brought GEO back online and had him analyze the egg all day."

"Good job. You look tired. I can handle the final sequencing from here," he replied.

"Thanks, I am going to bed," she said with a look of relief.

Doug turned to face the computer screen when Joan left. "Hello, GEO, how are you today?" Doug asked.

"Why quite fine, Dr. McDowell. How are you?"

"Great, are we ready to begin?"

"Yes, I have sequenced the DNA into my database and am prepared for the final sequence to fertilization. Please use the keyboard as voice command will be offline due to security programming."

Doug brought the keyboard in front of him and began to type in the necessary passwords and codes that would enable GEO to begin to fertilize another egg for a baby girl. It was a bit of a process though and it took a while to do. It prevented any unauthorized person from ever using the machine. He finally finished entering the codes. Now all he had to do was follow the computer screen prompt, which was: "Press any key to continue."

"Dr. McDowell!" Kirk came bursting in. "They are after Adam, come quickly!" He shoved a gun in Doug's hand.

"Who?!" Doug stammered.

"The Afim!" Kirk said.

Doug was horrified. "The Afim…here? My God!" Grasping the other man, he yelled, "Pam!"

"This way!" Kirk cried as the two ran down the hallway towards Pam's quarters.

P am was rocking the baby softly, singing to him. The baby was looking at Pam's face as she held him. A single hand went up to touch her face. *It is so little*, she thought. He probed Pam's face as she sung softly to him. She continued to rock him gently until he finally fell to sleep. She gently lay him down in the crib and covered him up with a blanket. She switched on the monitor, turned off the light and went into the other room. She grabbed a book off the shelf and a blanket and was going to sit in the chair when a crash came at the door.

The door flew open and in came one of the soldiers. Pam screamed. Then catching her breath and grinning, she said, "Whew, I thought you might be one of the enemy soldiers." She was about to give the man a lecture as well about knocking on doors before entering when she realized he held a knife in his hand.

The soldier grinned at her with a wicked smile as he lifted the rather large knife. He came at her swinging the blade, intent on falling his victim as quickly as possible.

Pam was no fighter, but she knew that there was a child in the other room. As she dodged the first swipe of the knife, something deep from within her kicked in.

It is a strange phenomenon that occurs when someone fights for their children. It has been well documented that regardless of strength, size or ability, a parent becomes a formidable and sometimes very dangerous enemy. This same instinct for life and the life of her baby came alive in Pam and like a bull she saw red.

He was backing her up, coming closer to her, but as she backed against the counter, she pulled one of the large beef-cutting knives out of the cutlery. It was razor sharp and bigger than the soldier's. She saw this, and so did he as a smug grin appeared on her face.

His grin faded as she rushed at him, swinging the knife. The sudden offensive caught the soldier by surprise as she slashed across his arm. He moved backward and she came at him again. But he was an experienced soldier not to be taken by just anybody. He was caught by surprise the first time, he would not be the second. He quickly brought his body down and his arm up, deflecting the brunt of her blow while with his other hand he slashed across hers, sending the knife she was holding sailing across the floor.

Sensing the finality of it, he came at her. His rush towards her propelled her backward, stumbling onto the floor. He was on top of her now, attempting to plunge the blade through her chest. But she grabbed his wrists as he tried to stab her. The knife was coming closer to her throat as his strength outweighed hers, and he began to bring the full weight of himself down upon her. He was grinning now as the knife began to touch the outermost skin of her neck.

Pam could feel the blade begin to pierce the skin as a drop of blood began to form at the tip where the knife was. She fought desperately against it, but he had his weight bearing down on it.

The man started to laugh when suddenly his whole body convulsed as several bullets ripped through his side, causing him to fall to the floor.

She looked around to see Kirk and Doug in the doorway. Breathing heavily, she lay on the floor. Doug ran to her and, picking her up, held her tight. She started to cry as she told him what had happened in between sobs.

"The baby, my baby!" she cried.

"He's okay," Kirk said. "Still sleeping."

"Oh thank God!" She let out a heavy sigh of relief. "I don't know what I would have done, I love him so much." Then, looking up at Doug, she said, "And I love you too! My hero!" She hugged him close.

"And I love you too. I am so glad you are all right," he said as he held her, feeling reassured that she was safe.

"Hey there, Pam, if you ever want a job, you just give me a call," Kirk said, grinning. He was relieved that she was okay, but also impressed with the way she had held her own for so long.

"Let's get them out of here," Doug said, as they all began to rise up.

Kirk went to the nearby communications board and instructed security to come down, clean up and move them.

However, as he was speaking and everyone was catching their breath, nobody noticed that the Afim soldier wasn't dead yet. As they were going on, he reached into the inner folds of his shirt and pulled out his gun and aimed it at the nearest person.

Pam was the first to see and screamed as Kirk in an instant shot around with his machine gun and pumped the man full of lead.

Everything in Pam's life at that moment moved in slow motion. Like when a person is watching a movie and they slow it down to catch it all in detail. Slowly, she saw the man's arm holding the gun fall to the floor with his hand still clutching it. She watched it bounce off of the floor from the impact and come back down again. She saw the flash from the gun barrel when it hit the floor, sending a shot off wildly.

They all ducked, and as they got up, they all saw the direction the gun was pointed.

Not a sound in heaven or earth could describe the scream of terror and disbelief that came from Pam's mouth at that moment. It was a sound that would freeze a person to the bone with pure horror. "NO!" she screamed, as they all ran into the baby's room.

The shot had gone right through the side of the crib. "Oh my God, my God!" Doug yelled as the baby was covered in blood, gasping for breath. Kirk went to the monitor, trying to get help while Doug went into the hallway to yell for help in the chance there might be a medical person nearby.

The hands of the baby were jerking uncontrollably and then suddenly, with one final shake, they fell. His eyes became glassy and slowly they closed.

That would be the last thing Pam would ever see. Somewhere, somehow, between the light and the darkness in her head, Pam entered that grey place to which she would never return.

Doug was slumped down next to the crib as he was sobbing. He and Kirk stayed there what seemed like an eternity. Finally, Doug picked up Pam in his arms and carried her out and began to make the ascent to the surface. He had lost everything and except for the possibility to help Pam, who was beyond all hope, he had nothing to hope for.

Kirk covered the child with a blanket as he, too, had been crying. All his training, all his work, seemed like so much bullshit now. All the flag waving and the duty honor meant nothing when you were looking at a dead little boy. He couldn't even save a child, a baby. When the people of Earth had brought war to their children, it was over, all over.

Another klaxon alarm sounded. It was a warning of intruders. Kirk got up and, grabbing his gun, fled down the corridor, almost bumping directly into Bass. Apparently, the general had come out of his stupor and wanted to be briefed. Kirk told him the whole story.

The general looked down and muttered, "...all my fault."

"No, sir, it's not your fault, it's mankind's fault," Kirk said as he put his hand upon the general's shoulder.

The general got his composure again as another alarm went off. John and Kirk knew what it was. That troops that were supposedly routed had somehow recovered, beaten their forces and penetrated the mountain. It was only a matter of time now.

They both sat down and the general opened his coat and pulled out a small flask and took a good slug. He then offered it to Kirk, who smiled and took some of the alcohol as well. They passed it back and forth until they had drained every drop.

The general now looked at him and said, "Well, Major, are you ready to perform one last duty?"

Kirk looked at him and gave him a half smile of admiration. "Yes, sir," he replied and fell into step behind him.

They walked down the corridors until they had got to a secured room. Walking inside, they closed and locked the door behind them. The general walked up to a terminal and put his hand on the monitor as the scanner scanned his handprint. The computer granted him security access as two massive doors in front of them slid open.

It was a small room with a computer terminal and two keyholes.

The general took a key out from under his shirt and Kirk took one out as well. "Enable destruct sequence," the general said.

Kirk put his hand on his switch and the general on his. "Three, two, one," and the two flipped their switches to set mode. The computer screen lit up and a warning sounded.

"Warning! Destruct sequence activated. One more turn to initiate self-destruct. To cancel, simply turn the key back," the computer voice said.

"Sir?" Kirk said, looking at the man whom he had come to respect and admire.

John Bass turned to look at the man. Kirk brought up a stiff salute to him. The general eyed him for a second and slowly brought up a salute in return. They both stood there for a moment. Then the general counted. Both men had their hands on the keys. "Three, two, one...."

The explosion that went out rocked the very foundation of the earth.

Chapter 28

"You see?" the old man said to the visitor through the monitor. "While I was busy in committees and doing all this advising, all of this was going on. They hunted for a while for survivors but the once mountainous countryside was now flattened land, and it left little to look for.

"As with so many of our wars, this one too eventually ended. It seemed that the forces of the Eastern Alliance were eventually beaten back into submission and a cease-fire accord was brought up.

"Once news about the child came out, there were trials brought about on the Earth to hold all those accountable. Polov was one of the many. He was found in his stateroom where he had hung himself.

"It seemed that after all of this, once man had finally destroyed his future, a peace came about on the Earth that has never occurred until that point. It would seem that it took our final realization of global destruction to finally make peace." The old man looked at the camera with a slight smile as if to say farewell to an old friend. "We all say goodbye now. Pass on our story, our legacy, and learn from it." At that, the monitor went dark.

The visitor thought a moment and slowly turned off the machine.

The other had been standing behind the visitor for some time, catching part of the documentary. He said to him, "Do you think there will ever be a race like them again?"

"I don't know," he replied.

Epilogue

Somewhere deep under tons of bedrock, there exists part of a tunnel and a small laboratory. Both are still intact. And in that laboratory is a computer and on the screen it waits patiently for a response to its prompt: "Press any key to continue."